THE WITCH WHO KILLED CHRISTMAS

A WONKY INN CHRISTMAS SPECIAL

JEANNIE WYCHERLEY

The Witch Who Killed Christmas
A Wonky Inn Christmas Special

BY
JEANNIE WYCHERLEY

Sign up for Jeannie's newsletter: http://eepurl.com/cN3Q6L

The Witch Who Killed Christmas was edited by Anna Bloom @ The Indie Hub
Cover design by JC Clarke of The Graphics Shed.

CONTENTS

CHAPTER ONE

I t must have been the cold that woke me.

Or perhaps the incessant tapping on my bedroom window.

Shivering, and imagining that the bedclothes must have somehow fallen from me in the middle of the night, I sat up. Nope. My covers were intact. I struggled upright, yanking the arms of my pyjamas down and shuddering at the biting cold that ran icy fingers around my neck as the duvet pooled around my middle.

Tap, tap, tap.

Blinking sleepily into the oddly pale glow that promised a bland dawn beyond the window, I tossed the bedclothes fully back, swinging my feet onto bare wooden boards. Most of the inn was habitable and beautiful now, after many months of hard work, but obviously I had left my own quarters till last. No

1

curtains, no carpets, just necessities until everything else had been completed to my desired standard throughout the inn. My guests had to come first.

I crept on tip-toe to the window—more to keep my feet off the cold floor than in an effort to keep noise to a minimum—and peered down at Mr Hoo, my stalwart companion. A familiar, if ever a witch had one. Mr Hoo was a long-eared owl, who stood about a foot high, with mottled pale brown markings mixed with darker brown. His round brown face looked up at me. His black eyes bleak, and his hooked beak raised, ready to tap against the glass again if I didn't let him in immediately.

Until that moment, I don't think I had ever considered it possible for an owl to look cold. From handling him, I knew that Mr Hoo possessed the ultimate in nature's insulation; a thick cloud of down padding that wrapped around his body and enveloped him in cushiony heaven.

A layer of warmth I could only dream of at 5.55 am on a December morning.

Now he stood several inches deep in fresh white snow, and his eyes conveyed his shock at being so sorely inconvenienced by the weather, so early in the day, so unseasonable for this part of England.

I gaped at Mr Hoo in surprise, then peered

further afield. Just the previous afternoon hadn't I been remarking how mild the winter had been so far this year? And how kind the seasons were to grant me such an abnormally long Autumn? I'd used the clement weather to press on with both the internal and external decoration the inn so desperately needed. More to the point, I could have sworn that the long-range forecast had been for a damp but relatively warm Christmas.

So why then, as I stood in front of the window in my absurdly thin nightwear, could I see the ground sparkling with a foot of frost covered snow? And why in the near distance were the trees of Speckled Wood laden with the white stuff too? Something, somewhere had gone wrong.

Really wrong.

I groaned.

A snow storm on December 23rd?

Tomorrow Whittle Inn would be packed to the rafters with new arrivals. The majority of my guests had booked—months in advance in some cases—to spend a carefree holiday here in the depths of the countryside under my hospitality. The preparations were in full swing, and I had hoped we were on track for my first full-on festive season. I'd been praying it would be problem-free, after all a busy Christmas could make or break the reputation of my wonky inn.

Today I expected several large food and drink deliveries, plus extra wood and coal, not to mention Christmas crackers and novelties, and little gifts I intended to hand out to all the guests.

But if I knew rural England the way I was beginning to think I did, there was little chance of the delivery trucks making it out from the depot, to say nothing of getting them up the narrow and winding lanes even to the nearby village of Whittlecombe, let alone my inn.

Mr Hoo took umbrage at the length of time it was taking for me to answer his call, and rapped urgently on the glass once more.

I flung open the window, only to be rewarded by a bitter blast of freezing air against my face. Mr Hoo shot past, shaking tiny shards of brittle frost all over me. He landed gracefully on a bedpost, where he preened his feathers furiously and studiously ignored me as I jumped up and down in a bid to warm myself.

Reaching out to catch the frigid brass of the handle, I wrenched the window closed, but not before fresh flakes of snow fell onto my bare arm.

I peered out at the sky in dread. Even in the semi-darkness, it appeared ominously heavy.

This could spell disaster.

Not what I needed at Christmas!

"Alf?" The plaintive voice, piping unexpectedly close to my ear, startled me. I jumped up and banged my head on the boiler.

I rubbed my crown and scowled at Charity who stepped away when she caught the look on my face. "Why's it so cold, Alf?" she asked. She looked sweet, clad in pyjamas and a thick woollen jumper, with her normally spiky pink hair, abnormally flattened, and much warmer than I felt. Charity was my new hotel manager. I'd recently pinched her from The Hay Loft—the other inn in the village—and it was one of the best business decisions I'd made since taking over the inn.

"I can't get the boiler to work." I waved my spanner in her direction and she backed off to the doorway. Probably wise. I'd stepped into my shower expecting warm water and met only a frigid waterfall. I had dried myself off rapidly but now I was colder than a naked Siberian mammoth during the Ice Age. And about as warm-tempered. I'd been trying to fix the huge old-fashioned boiler, housed in its own little room next to the kitchen, for the past forty minutes and I wasn't getting anywhere.

"Brrr." Charity shivered.

"Brrr indeed." I glowered. "Have you seen outside?"

"Outside? No." Charity headed for the door and I quickly followed her into the kitchen.

"How about we just look at it from in here," I suggested, eager to keep what little warmth the draughty old building had inside where it would do the most good.

I clasped Charity's arm and woman-handled her to the window. We both stared out, agog at the rapidly deteriorating weather conditions. Snow fell relentlessly from a dull white sky.

"It's snowing!" Charity erupted with excitement. Einstein had very little to worry about where Charity was concerned. "That's incredible! I haven't seen snow in Whittlecombe for years! And never in December."

It's probably worth pointing out a few facts here. When Charity says she hasn't seen snow for years, you need to remember she's all of about twenty-four. Six years younger than me. However, what she said was true. With our proximity to the south coast, and therefore the prevailing jet stream, snow is always a rarity. Snow in December is virtually unheard of. It's usually far colder at the end of January and beginning of February, if it gets cold at all.

"Wow." Charity clapped her hands in glee. "So pretty!" She stopped when she caught my expression. "Oh."

"Yes, '*oh*'. What am I going to do?" I asked. "Do you think the pipes are frozen? Maybe that's why the boiler isn't working?" Charity grimaced and shrugged, plumbing not being her forte, nor mine come to that. "What time is it now?"

That was a question she could answer. "Just after eight."

"Eight? That's almost civilised, isn't it? Could you call a plumber for me, please? There's a number in the book in the office. Under P. For plumber. I can't remember his name. Henry, or Eddie or...something."

"No probs," Chastity replied, and skipped away. I returned my attention to the boiler and prodded a few buttons, pulled a few levers, and depressed a switch, praying the darn thing would ignite. But when Chastity padded back into the kitchen a few minutes later, I'd still had no joy, and was considering taking a hammer to the decrepit old machine and smashing it to bits. How much would a new boiler cost me?

"It's Perry," Chastity announced. "Perry the plumber."

"Great. And will Perry come out in this weather?" I dropped my spanner into the toolbox with relief.

"Um, no. The phone's dead."

"The phone's dead?"

"No tone. Nada."

"You can't get a signal?"

"Ohhhhhh." Charity laughed with relief. "I didn't try a mobile. I just used the phone on your desk." My office housed a large Bakelite phone from the 1970s in matt black, complete with chrome rotary dial.

I shook my head in disbelief, but I had to laugh. Charity could be a dolt at times, but she was the most hard-working manager I could ask for. She had to put up with so much, after all.

It's easy to forget you're living in the twenty-first century in Whittle Inn. So many of the features, and a fair amount of the furnishings, date from a bygone era. This is both an aesthetic and a practical decision on my part. While the marketing we use attracts a number of 'traditional' guests from time-to-time, the bulk of reservations for my wonky inn are made up of witches, wizards, faeries, vampires and others of —shall we say—more mythical persuasion? You couldn't describe them all as evil or even particularly mischievous by any means, although some certainly are. However, I would admit, that on the whole my clientele are...well...weird.

And that meant that a large number of them liked to communicate via alternative means. Bakelite phone being one of their preferred methods, telegraph, owl, headless coachman and carrier pigeon among the others.

It all made sense to me.

"Try Perry the plumber on your mobile," I said, emphasising the word mobile sarcastically. "And keep trying if he's busy."

"'Kay."

"Thanks." I stretched and heard the satisfying crick of the bones in my neck. "I'm going to get dressed and go out and see what the lanes are like. Maybe organise the Wonky Inn Clean-up Crew to shovel snow." I gave the boiler one last kick.

"Alf?" Charity called after me as I headed for the stairs. "Can we ask the crew to light fires inside too?"

"Will do!" I yelled back. I expected Florence was already on to that anyway.

I headed for the attic.

Upstairs was far colder than downstairs. I don't have a clue how thatched roofs work, but I have always generally assumed they are naturally insulating— warmer in the winter and cooler in the summer. That didn't appear to be the case today. The air was positively icy in the rafters. My breath wheezed out in clouds of white steam.

The good thing about ghosts however, is that they don't feel the cold.

Nonetheless, when I opened the attic door I found them all huddled together, peering out of the circular window at the end of the attic, watching the falling snow with varying expressions on their pale and slightly opaque faces.

A stately looking woman turned to look at me as I entered. Alfhild Gwynfyre Daemonne, my great grand-mother, sported a diamond tiara and a navy blue velvet evening gown with matching gloves rolled up above her elbows. She didn't smile when she spotted me.

"This is a rum business," she said before I could greet her.

I narrowed my eyes at her. Her general predisposition for pessimism and doom and gloom had a tendency to set some of her fellow spirits off too, and given the day I was already experiencing, I wanted to avoid an outpouring of maudlin and melancholy where possible.

I'd had quite enough of sobbing ghosts for one year.

"Grandmama," I chastised, using the address she preferred. Behind her back I called her Gwyn. "It's just a bit of snow."

Before she could retort, and I could see she was poised to do so, I clapped my hands like a school ma'am. "Guys," I sang. "I'm sorely in need of your help this morning."

The motley collection of ghosts turned their attention to me. "Zephaniah," I addressed a tall thin man with only one arm, dressed in a First World War soldier's outfit. "Can you gather the troops together, please? I need you to lay fires in every room that will be inhabited by guests from tomorrow, but can you prioritise the rooms we will use today. Light the fires in communal areas, but hold off on the others. I need you to make sure the fires remain well-stoked, all day. Understood?"

"Yes ma'am!" Zephaniah shot back at me, and clicked his heels.

"Then when that's under control," I continued, "Can you get a crew outside and shovel snow? Start in the drive—"

"Oh but it's so pretty!" interjected Florence, a housemaid who had worked under my great great grandparents and who had met her end when her clothes caught alight. Even now, she smouldered all day long, and I could smell her before I would see her.

"I know it is, Florence, but we have to be practical. I'm expecting some big deliveries today. The vans won't make it up the lane unless we give them a helping hand."

"In my day—" Gwyn began, but I waved my hand at her.

"Do what you can to help everyone, Grand-mama, please?" I pleaded. "I'll check back with you all soon. I must head into the village."

I winked at Zephaniah, and shot back downstairs, ignoring the lamentations that followed me.

That's the problem with ghosts. They're so overly dramatic.

CHAPTER TWO

H ere in Britain, we find it hard to cope when the weather becomes a little extreme. Today was no exception. I donned a pair of old Wellington boots I'd found in the shed, pulled on an extra woollen layer, and a huge old mackintosh from the attic that smelled of mildew and old cologne, while regretting the fact I didn't have any of the right clothes of my own for this unseasonable turn of events.

By the time I left the inn, the scent of wood fires mingled pleasantly with the sharpness of the frosty air. Turning to observe my wonky inn with its thatched roof and numerous high brick chimney breasts, I watched the curls of grey smoke drift out against the milky background of the sky. A low sky that promised even more snow.

The snow itself was surprisingly deep and firm.

I'd been expecting loose powdery snow, the kind that melts at the slightest hint of sun, but I should have known better. The air was biting, and the cold seeped through my layers and settled into my bones. My feet sank into the snow, but only by a few inches. This stuff was hardcore.

I trudged down the lane, humming as I walked, keeping myself company, and trying to convince myself I felt warm enough. Once out on what passed for the main road into the village, I was struck by how silent everywhere was. Whittlecombe is a quiet village at the best of times, but there is always traffic of some kind. Locals on bicycles, or in their sports cars in some cases, jeeps and tractors from the local farms, delivery vehicles, sometimes even commuter traffic heading from hidden and remote hamlets to the city of Exeter, some 18 or so miles away.

But the lack of traffic noise wasn't what struck me the most. It was the total absence of animal noise, something as a witch I was usually finely attuned to. I paused in the middle of what was normally the road and cocked my head, stilling my breathing and listening hard. Not a tweet or a cheep. Not a rustle, snuffle or a grunt. No honking, no braying, no barking, no meowing.

Whittlecombe and surrounding areas appeared to be entirely devoid of animals.

Either that or they had holed up somewhere, and were busy keeping themselves warm.

I carried on down the road and into the village, pleased to see more life here. There were several locals gathered outside the community centre, including Mr Bramley who waved cheerily at me as he took a break from shovelling snow from the pavement there. I noticed the café had remained closed, but Whittle Stores was open, and busy enough. I made my way in, shaking the snow from my boots and coat and waving at Rhona and Stan behind the counter.

"Ah, hi Alf," Rhona called as she finished serving the woman in front of me. "I wondered whether you'd call in. We have several boxes to deliver to you today, but I'm not sure we're going to be able to get the van out."

"That's what I was worried about," I replied. "Won't the council get the snowploughs on the road?"

Stan shook his head. "Our phone lines are down, along with the broadband, so it's difficult to get any information. We've been trying to ring on Rhona's mobile, but we can't seem to get through."

"I guess they're very busy," Rhona interrupted.

"I'm sure they are." My stomach churned at the thought that I'd be losing customers if the roads weren't clear. In London, snow clearance and gritting etc., often seemed to happen automatically. I guess there were more resources allocated to a smaller area, compared to the county of Devon, which is vast. "Are they normally on the ball with this kind of thing?"

Stan shrugged. "It can be a bit hit and miss. You know how it is, limited resources. They start with the main routes out of the city, and concentrate on A roads, and larger towns."

That meant the tiny village of Whittlecombe would be well down the list. My heart sank.

"I caught the weather forecast on Breakfast TV," said Stan. "The presenter was forecasting more of the same. And what was especially weird? He couldn't explain where this weather front had suddenly come from. It just developed over the south west coast and it appears to be drifting inland."

"So they're forecasting more snow?" I asked.

"Followed by freezing rain. You know, they said it could be like the freezing ice storms they have in North America from time to time."

"Oh no!" I couldn't help my dismay. It looked

like my first wonky Christmas would have to be cancelled.

"Arr," Rhona drawled, seeing my face. "Chin up, Alf! You know what the British weather is like. All this will be gone tomorrow! It could be worse."

She'd hardly finished the sentence when the electricity went out.

The abrupt silence seemed oddly loud. The fridges and freezers clicked off, the lights died. The till went black. I could feel the absence of electronic vibration in the air.

"Now you've done it," Stan said quietly to his wife. "You were saying?"

Rhona opened her mouth to protest but then closed it again.

We stood looking at each other in the semi-darkness, waiting for the electricity to return. Nothing happened.

I closed the shop door to keep the warmth in. Rhona walked around to my side of the counter and turned the swinging door sign to 'closed'.

"This is not good," I said.

"No," she murmured. We stood together looking out of the window, glancing up and down the road. People started poking their heads out of dark cottages to check that everyone was in the same boat. Neighbours chatted to each other, and gestured towards the shop. The shop was the hub of the community and the community would pull together. I was glad of that.

"Do you have plenty of wood available for stoves?" I asked Rhona.

She thought for a moment, then nodded. "Some."

"Maybe you'd better ration it. What do you think? Make sure everyone who needs it has enough? With no electricity, some folk will have to rely on wood stoves as their only source of heat. Charge it to the inn if you have to, Rhona, if people are short of cash. I'll settle with you."

"Do you have plenty up there at the inn?"

"I have a pile in the wood store. Enough to last a few days if I'm careful. I was expecting an inn-full of guests over the next few days, so I had plenty in but was expecting a delivery. Unless this weather clears up, I probably won't see any guests anyway so I won't need all I have."

My stomach twisted again. Still, there was no point in feeling morose. I had to make the best of it. "As you say, it could be worse."

We smiled at each other and I prepared to take my leave.

Stan waved. "If the ploughs get through, I'll make sure you get what you need, Alf."

"Thanks, Stan, I appreciate it. And if this weather continues and you hear of anyone struggling to cook on Christmas day, send them up to the inn. I've an oil-fired range in the kitchen. We'll be eating well, whatever the weather!"

"By candlelight, maybe?" Rhona said and I laughed as though the idea was quite absurd.

Stepping outside, I made my way along the cleared pavement. Mr Bramble had been working hard. He winked at me as I went past and I complimented him on a good job well done, and told him not to overdo it. One glance at the low sky, heavy with the promise of more snow, convinced me poor Mr Bramble might be fighting a losing battle.

Heading back towards the inn took me past Hedge Cottage. One of the prettiest and snuggest cottages in the village, it belonged to my friend and fellow witch, Millicent Ballicott. It didn't surprise me in the slightest when she appeared on her doorstep and hailed me as I approached.

"What *are* you wearing?" she asked as I stamped up her drive.

I sniggered in amusement. Millicent, a well-cushioned lady in her early sixties, was not exactly renowned for her own fashion sense. Today she appeared to be wearing navy blue slacks, with a pair of rainbow coloured Nepalese woollen socks pulled over her trousers and coming up to her knees, along with several misshapen jumpers in varying shades of mustard and beige, and a Russian ushanka-hat with the earflaps down.

"This was all I could find at the inn that was suitable for the weather," I said. I pulled the wellies from my feet and left them in her porch before stepping into her warm living room. A fire burned brightly in the grate and she had a few candles in jars, providing a surprising amount of light in the dark cottage. The overall effect was cosy. Jasper, her large lurcher, lounged on the sofa. He wagged his tail lazily when he spotted me but didn't bother getting up. I wanted to throw myself down with him, cosy and warm, and demand we be served tea and cake, instead of heading back to the cold inn.

"I can't stop," I said reluctantly. "I've left Charity with the ghosts. Our boiler is out of action. Stan was just saying this weather is set to get worse."

"Yes," Millicent nodded. Her face grim. "About that."

"About the weather?"

"It's not right Alf."

I wanted to laugh. Well no. Of course it wasn't right, but it was December. December *is* winter in the northern hemisphere. It can snow. It has been known. But I knew Millicent, and she was no harbinger of doom without good cause. Besides, deep down, in my gut, I knew she was right.

"I heard about something like this, many years ago. This weather anomaly. It was on a smaller scale, but it didn't occur naturally."

"What caused it then?" I asked curiously.

"Maybe a witch or wizard gone rogue."

I did a double take. "A witch gone rogue? Really?" I couldn't imagine that one of our kind would have the power to single-handedly trigger a chain of catastrophic weather events and cause so much disruption. Unless...

"Not The Mori?" I asked. A cold knife sliced through my insides and I shivered. I'd hoped we had seen the last of The Mori after the Battle of Speckled Wood, my rude awakening at Whittle Inn earlier in the year.

"No," Millicent put her hand on my arm, patting

me like she might Jasper on Guy Fawkes night. "Not them."

"Oh. Thank goodness. You scared me then." I exhaled, releasing the tension I'd been holding. I'd nearly lost everything at their hands. I didn't want to face them again.

The wind rattled Millicent's old window panes and we both glanced outside. The sky was a slate grey and snow, as I had expected, had started to fall again. Poor Mr Bramble.

"I'm going to send a query to Wizard Shadow-mender, and remind him of an incident I've heard of in the past." Millicent was the witch version of neighbourhood watch. Forever writing letters to the local papers here in Devon, and the Council of Elders in London. "I'm sure he won't have forgotten. Then perhaps he can cast light upon this occurrence, and get back in touch with us."

"Alright," I said, turning for the door. "I really think I must get back." Unease spread through me; a heavy sensation of dread, a tingling that started on my scalp. Millicent was right, something was off with this weather.

"Alf, wait. Before you go, I want you to take this." She handed me a large bundle of clothing tied with thin rope.

"What's this? Clothes? Give them to a charity, Millicent, I don't need these."

"I have a feeling you do," Millicent said, and although she smiled, there was a glint of steely determination in her eyes.

CHAPTER THREE

My ghost crew had been working hard. The lane was partially cleared when I lugged Millicent's bundle up towards the inn. The snow threw itself down, unrelenting and heavy, and I turned the ghosts for home, struggling to follow them as they moved with ease ahead of me, leaving no tracks where they trod.

The main room of the inn was warm and cosy. A huge fire crackled in the grate with an enormous log burning in the centre of it. I shed my top layer by the front door and nodded at Zephaniah. "That's nice. Keep this fire going please, all day and all night for now," I said. "And ask Florence to make sure the range and the fire in the kitchen don't go out. We may have visitors from the village."

"Will do, Miss Alf." Zephaniah glided rapidly away with his new instructions.

Over at the bar, Charity was chatting to someone on her mobile. As soon as she finished the call, it rang again.

"Whittle Inn, good morning. Charity speaking, how may I help you today?" she sang. Then listened. "Oh, I'm sorry to hear that. Yes. Yes. Alright. We will hold your booking open of course, so if things improve just let us know you've changed your mind. We will. Thank you. And you. Merry Christmas!"

She put the phone down and stared balefully at me. "Sorry, Alf. Cancellation after cancellation. Our guests are finding it hard to leave their own homes, let alone travel into the depths of rural Devon. Is it really that bad out there?"

I blew my cheeks out, sighing heavily. "Yes. And it's set to get worse. Well, there is nothing we can do about it, Charity, apart from keep the bookings open. You never know, conditions may improve and people will change their minds at the last minute."

However, in my heart of hearts, I knew there was no hope of any festive frivolity this Christmas in my wonky inn.

I spent the rest of the morning taking an inventory of

the supplies we had available, on the off chance that guests did make it through, or we had visitors from the village. We had food enough to last a few days, including several turkeys hanging in the cold store and numerous other joints of meat in the deep freezer. I instructed these to be taken out to defrost and set Florence and her willing spirit kitchen helpers to begin prepping vegetables. Again, I had no shortage of frozen items, but I had expected the fresh ones to be delivered today and tomorrow.

"Do what you can with what we have," I said, with no choice but to leave her to it. We had candles and fuel and more or less everything we needed for 48 hours, but no gifts, no decorations, no fresh fruit or vegetables, milk or other dairy, and no chocolate, nuts or treats or clementines, which I personally considered particularly disastrous.

"It could be worse!" I repeated the mantra slightly hysterically, resisting the urge to rock back and forth in the corner of the room, remaining instead at the window in the bar for some time, so I could monitor the weather. The wind had increased in strength since I'd returned home. I could just about make out the trees that lined both sides of the lane. They bowed in the wind, first this way, then that, their bare branches shaking and dancing. One moment snow buffeted against the windows, then when the wind changed direction, and the snow sped away from me. I could see drifts beginning to build. The path the ghosts had cleared earlier had already been covered over.

Florence offered me a steaming bowl of leak and potato soup for lunch. I sat in an armchair, by the fire, and watched as the flames twisted one way and then another, caught by random draughts, before they leapt up the chimney. The soup warmed me through, and my body slowly melted into the leather of the armchair. Lulled into comfort I placed my tray on the floor, and closed my eyes.

I must have fallen asleep because I was startled out of my reverie by a falling log. Zephaniah appeared by my side and scooped the burning log up, flinging it back into the fire with his one available ghost hand.

"Careful," I said, although I knew he couldn't feel pain.

I blinked and stretched. The wind howled around the building, whistling through cracks in the wood of the doors, window frames and floors. Whittle Inn is an old building, structurally sound, but definitely not air-tight. "What time is it?"

Outside the sky hung dark and dense, an impenetrable blanket, and it was impossible to guess.

"About four." Ah, that would be right. The shortest day in the calendar year had only just been and gone.

"This came for you, ma'am." Zephaniah indicated a brown parcel wrapped with string, on the floor by the hearth. It was a box, about 12 inches square.

"Somebody brought this up the lane?" I asked, my hopes soaring for a moment. *Deliveries were getting through?*

"Not exactly. There was a tap on the door, and this had been left on the step outside..."

"But no-one was there?" I finished for Zephaniah.

He nodded. "No, ma'am."

I picked up the box, surprisingly light for such a solid looking object. Perhaps a jumper from Millicent. But no, turning the box first one way then the other to inspect it, I could only watch as the cord that bound it undid itself like a snake untying its own knots, then dropped to the floor. I pulled the paper off. Inside I found a plain white box. Lifting the lid exposed newspaper shavings. I shook them into the fire until I uncovered a snow globe.

Ostensibly it was a snow globe. As soon as I moved it, snow billowed inside the glass. But I instantly recognised the item for what it actually was. An orb. A scrying orb. I'd seen Wizard Shadowmender using one.

My mouth dropped open. After a lifetime of largely ignoring any of my witchy skills and powers, I had only recently re-subscribed to the lifestyle and begun working with the craft once more. I had endeavoured to learn and practise as much as I could, but I had a long way to go to meet even minimum proficiency. Shadowmender's extraordinary gift clearly demonstrated his faith in me. More than I had in myself probably.

I hoped I could live up to his belief.

The question therefore appeared to be whether there was a link between the orb and Millicent's message to him? Where Shadowmender was concerned, it seemed unlikely that the two factors were a mere coincidence.

I turned the orb upside down and righted it again. Once more a blizzard swirled within the glass, but this time as it began to clear I thought I could make out trees. I turned the orb on its side, twisted it about, catching the firelight, enabling me to see more clearly.

Definitely trees.

And a small wooden cabin.

I held the orb still, but the snow exploded again, obscuring my view. I turned it upside down once more, watching the flurry go crazy, then righted it and let it settle. Quite clearly I could see the cabin, and a tiny prick of light. When I moved, the light disappeared.

I held the glass orb still in front of my eyes and turned myself around. Then again. And back once more. The light could only be seen when I faced a certain way. It glowed like a tiny star in a dark sky, within the miniscule world it inhabited in the orb. I walked forwards, heading through the kitchen where Florence was busily making a crumble, and towards the back door. I opened the back door. The snow had drifted and piled high against it, so I didn't venture outside, but I could clearly see the light in the orb glowing more brightly when I held it in the direction of Speckled Wood, the private wood I owned located behind the inn.

Shadowmender had quite clearly sent a message.

I had to follow the star.

CHAPTER FOUR

"Y ou're not intending to go out in that?" Charity's incredulous voice followed me back into the bar.

"I am," I replied, walking away from her. "I have to."

Charity paused in the doorway, her hands on her hips, slowly shaking her head. "You have to? There's a little light in a snow globe and you think you need to follow it? I've heard some crazy things in my time, most of them since coming to work at the inn with you, but that pretty much takes the biscuit."

"Look." I handed the orb over to her, and she took it in both hands, tipping it gently, left and right. "It's not a snow globe."

"I can see snow in it." She shook it harder and watched the blizzard clear. "Oh. Wait. You're right.

There's no liquid like you would usually see. It's more like..." Charity screwed her face up. "Like a fortune teller's ball or something."

"A crystal ball. Yes. That's pretty much what it is," I replied, heading for the entrance where I had abandoned my mackintosh and wellingtons. Millicent's fat bundle caught my eye. I tugged at the rope she had bound the clothes with and watched what unrolled. A downy snow jacket in dark green had been wrapped around heavy waterproof trousers, snowshoes, thick wool socks, a thick multi-coloured fleece cardigan with a matching scarf and hat, a thermal vest, thermal leggings, and a waterproof rucksack. I stared with interest at the miscellany of items.

Had Millicent known in advance that I needed to go on a journey? Why hadn't she said so?

I pulled the items apart and held up the leggings and vest. My size. Not Millicent's size. The trousers were a size too large, as was the snow jacket, but given the number of layers I'd be wearing, they would fit me perfectly. This collection of oddities would be far better suited for this weather than the overlarge gents' rain coat I had been sporting earlier, and the ancient wellies from the shed.

I opened the rucksack. Empty apart from a torch. I checked the batteries. They were working. There were no other clues as to what I should be doing or where I should be going.

Charity joined me. "Where did this lot come from?"

"Millicent."

Charity sniffed. Then folded her arms and regarded me obstinately. "She's in on this too, is she? I see."

I hid a smile. Charity was part of the mundane life of the village, a mortal with no supernatural powers. She managed the inn, and to a large extent me, very well. She took the weirdness that encompassed our daily lives completely in her stride. Initially wary of the ghosts, she now treated them as friends – and irritants – which seemed an altogether healthy way of dealing with them to my mind. She remained polite, courteous and professional to our guests at all times, regardless of who they were or what their peculiar penchants and peccadillos might be.

She rarely drew a line, but I could see from the scowl on her face, and the worry in her eyes, that this whole situation was troubling her.

"You can't go out there in this. I mean, look outside. You can't see your hand in front of your face. It's a white out." She glared at me. "It will only get colder overnight, and you said yourself, freezing rain is forecast. I won't let you go."

I turned to stare out of the nearest window. There was nothing to be seen now. The bottled panes of glass rattled in their frames, and behind me the fire stuttered and spat, casting long shadows against the walls.

"I suppose you're right," I said reluctantly.

Charity narrowed her eyes at me and I shrugged innocently. "Why don't you take this upstairs and dump it on my bed," I said to her, collecting together everything except the coat, boots and rucksack and handing it over. "I'm going to give Florence a hand with dinner."

"You're sure you're not going anywhere?" Charity demanded, heading for the stairs.

"Not in this. Not tonight. You're right," I nodded, appeasing her. I watched her climb the stairs until she was out of sight, then picked up the rucksack and the orb and quickly headed for the kitchen.

"Florence," I called, and the ghostly house maid whirled about merrily. She was in her element in the kitchen, and loved helping out when our grumpy French chef would let her. I held up the rucksack. "I need you to fill this up with supplies. A hot thermos of soup. Perhaps one of tea. Some water. Snacks. Sandwiches. Anything to keep me going on a long walk."

"Yes, milady," Florence bobbed a curtsey.

I lowered my voice and glanced at the kitchen door, half expecting my hotel manager to reappear. "Hide the bag for now, and make sure Charity doesn't see it," I instructed. "Leave it on the kitchen table after we've all turned in." Florence looked startled but I knew she would do as I asked. "And, Florence," I hissed. "Don't tell anyone else about this."

I tried to behave normally for the rest of the evening, idling the time away until I could head up to bed. Given the lack of electricity, and therefore with no TV or radio to entertain us, it was easy to excuse myself to retire early, and head upstairs to join Mr Hoo.

I quietly pushed my bedroom door closed, but left it off the latch. I intended to make an early getaway and I didn't want anyone else in the house to be disturbed.

Florence had organised tea light candles in all the bedrooms. They gave off a warm glow in my room, and a fire had been lit in here too. I sagged with relief as I turned away from the door, congratulating myself on not further alerting Charity to my plans.

I nearly jumped out of my skin when I realised I was not alone.

Gwyn stood by the fire, regarding me with suspicion.

"Grandmama!" I yelped. "You made me jump!"

"Well you really shouldn't be skulking around," she retorted.

I shouldn't have been surprised. My father's formidable grandmother could often be found in my suite of rooms, otherwise known as the owner's apartment, comprising a bedroom, a tiny kitchen, a wonderful old Victorian bathroom and an office. During her lifetime, she had slept in exactly this room, in my very bed. I regularly awoke to find her sleeping on the other side of my bed.

To be fair, it is difficult to banish your great grandmother from her own bed, even if she has been dead for the best part of seventy or so years.

"Why haven't you gone?" she demanded, rather too loudly for my liking.

"Ssshhh!" I hissed and flapped my hands, indicating the door. Charity slept on the fourth floor, but she could go past my door to reach the back staircase if she chose.

"Oh really," Gwyn retorted. "You're such a worry wort."

"Grandmama," I squeezed my hands together in a plea. "Please keep your voice down." Gwyn arched an eyebrow and pursed her lips. I took this as acquiescence as she sat on the bed and I paced nervously around the room. Mr Hoo, balancing on the bedpost watched me through wide interested eyes.

"Gone where?" I asked. "Where exactly am I going?" Gwyn folded her arms obstinately. "Tell me what you know about all this." I kept my tone as low as I could manage while trying to fiercely demand information. When it looked like she wouldn't answer, I wagged my finger at her and then the door, indicating she should leave. I knew this would get a reaction. We often argued about whether the bedroom was hers or mine.

She tutted. "Really, Alfhild. It's rude to point."

"Why did you ask me why I hadn't left?" I asked

quietly. "How do you know I'm going somewhere?" I caught myself. "Or might be."

"You are."

"Let's just say, I might be. Possibly. For the sake of argument. What do you know?"

CHAPTER FIVE

Sometime before five the following morning I let myself out of the back door of the inn, into the relative stillness of a new day. Wearing my rucksack on my back, I tucked the orb down the front of my jacket. Getting dressed, I'd feared I wouldn't be able to move given the number of layers I needed to wear, but Millicent had turned out to be a genius in the clothing department, and I had freedom of movement combined with a steady warmth from my thermal layer.

Long may that continue, I thought as I closed the door carefully behind me.

The woodpile to the left of the door caught my eye. Usually covered by a tarpaulin, I could see the corner sticking up where the wind had blown against it, exposing the axe on the block. Without thinking, I hoisted the axe in my right hand, settled the torch in my left, and headed for Speckled Wood.

With no idea how far I needed to go, for now I turned my face towards the dawn and headed away from the comfort and safety of the inn.

I wasn't surprised to hear the stealthy beating of wings overhead a little later. Mr Hoo would never let me journey very far without his company, and never when I headed into the wood. He flew on ahead and settled on branches to wait whenever I was slow to catch up.

I averted my eyes when I came to the clearing where I, along with Wizard Shadowmender and our friends, had bested The Mori, at least temporarily. I banished memories of Jed, the man I had fallen in love with, and kept on moving, concentrating on my footing, and where I was going, in the dim light of the forest.

Snow cover seemed patchy in the wood. It had drifted against the trees in certain places, and yet the paths had been scoured clean by the wind in others. I stuck to the path where possible, because I knew it would take me all the way through the wood. My wood.

Where my wood ended and the forest began, that's where my troubles really started.

Moving out of Speckled Wood and into the forest beyond was like stepping into another world.

Dawn was breaking as I transitioned, and the light improved to such an extent that I could stow my torch in my rucksack. I kept a careful eye out for wildlife, tracks or sounds, but there was nothing. How could this part of Devon seem so remote?

The still countryside unnerved me even with the beat of Mr Hoo's wings close by. I felt anxious and alone not knowing what or whom I was up against, or what I would find. I considered turning back, but thoughts of Wizard Shadowmender kept me moving forwards. He had gifted me the orb. Surely he wouldn't have packed me off alone if he didn't think I could cope with whatever was coming.

Perhaps food or drink would make me feel better? I'd yet to have breakfast and I needed to keep my strength up. I considered taking a drink from my thermos but I knew if I finished the tea this early in my travels, I'd be kicking myself before long.

I paused long enough to pull out the orb and take stock of my surroundings. Holding the orb up at eye level, once the snow had cleared from within the glass, I could clearly see the wooden cabin. The tiny star glowed brightly when I continued along the same direction I was taking, so I kept going.

There were fewer coniferous trees in this part of the forest. The branches of the tall oaks, and beeches, the ashes and the silver birches, were silhouetted spikily against an increasingly bleak sky. There was a deeper covering of snow here too, with less of a canopy to prevent the snow falling on the forest floor.

My feet crunched through the snow, and occasionally I skidded on patches of icy puddles. Here and there I found more slippery areas where water had frozen on top of the snow, more places where my feet made sharper cracking sounds as I placed my weight on the snow. My cheeks burned as the cold wind slashed across my face, and I paused to reposition my scarf. Normally I hated having anything covering my mouth, but now I was desperate to keep myself warm.

Thirty minutes later a strange noise halted me in my tracks. It reminded me of glass bottles, hung together in a line, glancing daintily off each other, like a wind chime. But this sound originated in the trees above my head. In confusion, I peered up through the twisted branches, but I couldn't see any bottles.

I walked closer, in among foliage draped lower to the ground, and I realised what the sound was. Not bottles at all, but solid ice, coating the branches above my head. When the breeze lifted, the branches clinked together, naturally melodic.

It could have been a pretty sound. Somehow festive. The chinking of champagne glasses at a party. But to me, as it rang through the silent forest, it jibed in the stillness and reverberated around the sentinel trees. A forewarning to something or someone. Portentous.

No. I found the sound purely ominous.

I had intended to stop at 9.30 to drink some tea, and eat something, but the going had become ever more difficult. The snow was hard, a thick coating of ice covering it everywhere now. Even with Millicent's rough terrain boots I was struggling to keep my footing, and falling on several occasions. Once or twice I'd come across deep drifts of snow and by mistake had walked into them and found myself knee deep in powdery snow, jarring a knee or an ankle when I miss stepped.

The landscape was changing too, the hills

becoming steeper the further away from the coast I ventured. This was new territory and I didn't know where I was, or indeed where I was heading. I could only trust my instincts, and every now and again, take the orb out from beneath my jacket and hold it up to catch the star. When I did, I'd begin moving forwards again, wondering at the futility of what I was doing.

And all for what? Because Millicent, Wizard Shadowmender and my great grandmother thought someone was playing with Mother Nature?

My breath laboured in my chest, my heart pounded, as I placed one foot in front of the other and hauled myself up another steep hill, reaching out for tree trucks, branches, anything solid enough to bear my weight and help me to keep me going.

To compound matters, tiny shards of icy rain fell out of the leaden sky, seeming to target any exposed areas of my skin. I tried to duck my head away from them, but that meant I couldn't see where I was going as I climbed yet another hill. I pulled my hat lower down over my eyebrows, leaving only my eyes exposed, but as I did so, I stepped into a drift once more. Mr Hoo called a warning but it was too late.

For a long moment, I seemed to float in the air. I lashed out, attempting to grab a branch at shoulder height, but it snapped off with a sharp crack, brittle in its frozen state. I braced myself, imagining I would turn my ankle again, or jar my knee, but the ground didn't come to meet me.

Not immediately.

The tangles of trees, frozen undergrowth, foliage and roots hid a sharp drop. I tumbled forwards, rolling down, crushing saplings and bushes as I went. I seemed to fall for an age until I whacked the ground, landing on my right hip and smacking my chin on the ground.

I lay stunned and winded for a moment, waiting for the pain to kick in, convinced I must be badly hurt. I was certain I would die here, alone. No-one knew where I was or how to find me. I'd seen those survival movies where someone breaks their leg and ends up cutting it off so they can ward off infection. Or they wait for help and get eaten by wolves. Yes, I thought dramatically, all that could and would happen to me.

Undoubtedly it would.

Mr Hoo fluttered down next to me, landing on a gate post.

"You'll have to go for help." I clutched my chest, aware I was being dramatic. The pain radiated out from the centre of me. "I'm finished."

"Hoo-ooo. Hoo-ooo."

"What do you mean?" I quizzed him. "Did you say we're here?"

Mr Hoo stared at me through his huge black eyes, then lifted one of his legs up, and deliberately, dropped it. When he did it the second and third time, I took in the gate post he was standing on.

Clever owl.

A gate meant an entrance. I was certainly somewhere.

Gingerly I sat up, everything appeared to be working pretty much as normal. I rubbed my chin, then patted my chest. The orb was still in one piece but had punched me in the centre of my ribs, between my breasts. That explained the ache. I was going to have some impressive bruises.

My rucksack flopped loosely to one side, so I shook it off. The left side strap had snapped, and no doubt my sandwiches were crushed inside. I turned about and gazed in awe at the steep slope behind me, an almost vertical drop of around twenty feet. I'd been lucky.

But Mr Hoo was right. Ahead of me, up a steep incline I could see the wooden cabin. My destination.

I just had to make the final 200 yards or so.

So near and yet so far. Those 200 yards were easier said than done.

I sat on a rock and drank some tea, pondering on the challenge still awaiting me. My legs felt like lead. I wasn't sure I had the energy to actually move again now I had stopped. Yet sitting and thinking wasn't an option. I was at the bottom of what—for all intents and purposes—was a large bowl-shaped hole.

Meanwhile, the tiny cabin was surrounded by twenty feet or so of thick undergrowth, a tangle of sturdy bushes, brambles, branches and tree roots that seemed to rise out of the ground to create an impenetrable barrier. I had only two ways out of the hole. Climb back the way I had arrived, so abruptly, then try and go around; or go through.

I limped over to where this natural barrier started, and peered at it, hoping to find an inlet of some kind, or path.

Nothing.

I skirted the edge. First one way and then the other, wondering if I could climb up the side, but no deal. I was trapped. My only solution would be to fight my way through.

I finished my tea, and hefting my axe began

glumly hacking a path through the wild web. It was slow going. The brambles tore at my coat. The twisted roots reached for my ankles. I realised I needed to chop halfway up each obstacle first, reaching forwards from waist height and attack there. Then I needed to back myself up, bend right over and have a go at the roots. The process took time, and exhausted the limited energy I had left. Slowly but surely—inch by painful inch—I travelled forwards. Brambles snagged in my hair and scratched my face. Thorns gripped my jacket and trousers, taking aim at my eyes, until finally, with a supreme explosion of energy on my part, I propelled my way through the last foot, tearing a hole in my coat when I yanked my way free once and for all.

I dropped the axe and sprawled spread-eagled onto the frozen ground, practically weeping through the exertion of what I had done.

An angry shriek split the silence of the afternoon. I looked up, eyes wide with fear and surprise, and came face to face with the furious and jabbering Mara the Stormbringer.

"Show me the orb," Gwyn had said the previous

evening, and I had reluctantly placed it on the bed for her to examine. She made a small gesture with her hands and it rose in the air, hovering in the space between us, so that we could both examine the contents.

"I thought so." She pulled her mouth down in disapproval.

"You thought what, Grandmama?"

"Mara."

I sighed in exasperation. "What does that mean? What is Mara?"

"It's not a what, it's a whom." Gwyn frowned at me as though I was a complete simpleton.

"I'm afraid you've lost me. Who is Mara? A friend of yours?" I scoured the orb for clues, but I couldn't see a figure in the orb, just the wooden cabin, surrounded by snow and tall trees. Peering closely, I could make out a thin curl of black smoke rising above the frozen roof. The cabin was inhabited then—presumably by this Mara person.

"In my day, way back in the twenties and thirties-"

When you were already getting on a bit, I thought but didn't dare say, of course.

"Alfhild," my great grandmother reprimanded me as though she could read my mind. I smiled innocently. "As I was saying, back in my day, Mara was a child. A young, pretty thing. An exceptional student. Brilliant in so many ways, come to think of it. Intelligent. She ran rings around all of her contemporaries. A stunning beauty, she turned the boys' heads, but she never did settle down with anyone. Totally dedicated to her craft."

"So what went wrong?" I asked, sitting on the bed. It was an assumption on my part, but let's face it, Devon found itself gripped in the middle of an iron winter, Shadowmender had sent me an orb, Millicent had loaded me up with weather-appropriate clothing, and now my great Grandmother felt the need to tell me a story? Yes, something, somewhere was very wrong.

"I don't know for sure. For many years she seemed happy enough, taught at the school on Celestial Street, gave lectures around the world, she even sat on the Council of Elders for a time. But she was always headstrong. Passionate. Somewhere along the line, her emotions began to affect her magickal practice."

I blinked. This was a new one on me. "Her emotions? How so?"

"Well think about it, Alfhild." I straightened at Gwyn's stern reprimand. "What is magick except the flow of energy into the world, directed by the practitioner?"

I nodded, seeing what she was getting at. "Of course. And the practitioner influences that energy flow."

"There's the magick that we all do when we hardly think about what we're doing. The way you direct your ghosts, or attend to the washing up, and so on."

"But you can be more involved." I thought back to how the Curse of Madb had been used against the intruder at the inn the day I moved here.

"Exactly. If you immerse yourself in magic, feel it, you can forcefully redirect it. However, that level of absorption will loosen your grip on reality and may cause you to lose all sense of self. It's a catch-22. You become disconnected from reality, and increasingly deeply immersed. The magick you can create can be some of the most powerful, but also the most dangerous."

I frowned. "So Mara became...what? Too emotionally involved in her magick?"

"Worse. Her emotions began dictating her magick. She didn't seem to have much control over what she was doing."

"And what was she doing?"

"Well, let's put it this way, her nickname is Mara the Stormbringer. Whenever she became angry, there would be a localised storm."

I conjured a picture in my head of a woman with a black raincloud above her head, remembering cartoons I'd seen of such a thing as a child, and giggled.

"Really, Alfhild, it is no laughing matter. A storm while out walking for leisure is one thing. A storm inside the chamber where the Council of Elders meet, or in a University lecture theatre or a school classroom, is something quite different."

I straightened my face. This is what Millicent had alluded to earlier. She must have heard about the incidents involving Mara. "You're right. I can see it would be a major inconvenience. I can't believe this wasn't addressed at the time though, Grandmama."

"Oh it was. Some of the greatest magickal doctors of the time attended to Mara, and I believe a number of esteemed magickopsychologists were consulted too. Things certainly improved for a while."

"What happened after that?"

"She moved away. Retired young. And I died, so

I'm not really up-to-date with what she's been doing for the past sixty years or so."

Point taken. I squinted into the orb. "But you think this is where she lives? Why?"

"I can't really tell you why, Alfhild. I don't know." Gwyn contemplated the orb thoughtfully for a moment, then added softly, "It's just intuition. Of all the witches I have encountered, she had the most extraordinary power when it came to creating weather anomalies. I don't know that one witch can be held responsible for what we're seeing at the moment, I truly don't. But I do know that Mara was a woman with extraordinary depth of emotion. If any witch had the power to conjure up a winter storm that could kill Christmas, it would be her."

I regarded my great grandmother with renewed interest. It was easy for me to be irritated by the ghosts who inhabited the inn at times, particularly those outside the Wonky Inn Clean-up Crew whom I had little control over, such as Gwyn, the chef Monsieur Emietter, and the bard, Luppitt Smeatharpe. It seemed beholden on me to remember that Alfhild Gwynfyre Daemonne had been renowned in magickal circles in her day. Millicent had told me that Gwyn had been a formidable witch in her own right.

Mr Hoo cooed gently behind us as he preened his feathers, the fire glowed, and I felt a rush of affection for my departed ancestor.

I smiled. "Well that's good enough for me, Grandmama. I'll see if I can find her." I indicated Mr Hoo, fluffed up and sleepy on the edge of my bed. "We'll leave before it gets light."

CHAPTER SIX

Mara's high-pitched shriek froze my blood as it ripped through the dead silence of the afternoon. Under any normal circumstances the surrounding forest would have erupted with the sound of animals bolting and birds taking to the wing, but even after the echo of her ferocious screech had faded away, there was no sound other than the glassy clink of frozen branches above our heads.

She and I might have been the only two living beings on a dead planet.

Of indeterminate age, but at least eighty, I judged, she was small and slight, under five feet in height. Hair long and grey; greasy. That about summed her up. She did not look like a woman who had taken care of herself for a long time. Her pallor was the colour of sour milk, her robes old and patched, nothing more than filthy rags. Her movements were anxious, characterised by nervy twitches, dark eyes darting here and there. She exuded an air of bitterness. Of ancient anger, directed at a harsh unforgiving world.

Her cold demeanour, and nervousness increased my own feeling of unease. I couldn't be sure I was safe with her.

Not taking my eyes from the elderly witch, I pushed myself up to my knees and raised my hands in surrender. "Mara?" I asked, keeping my voice as calm as I could manage. I didn't want to alarm her, although the fact I was frightened to death myself, seemed to mitigate against this.

"Who wants to know?" she demanded, striking the tall stick she was wielding against the snow at her feet. The very ground around me vibrated with the thrust. I placed my hands on the cold compacted surface to attempt to steady myself.

"My name is Alfhild Daemonne. I live at Whittle Inn, in Whittlecombe, just a few miles south west of here. You may not know it. I've been walking all day." I indicated the treacherous conditions.

"No-one asked you to," she spat. "So why have you come?"

"May I stand?" I asked. She didn't reply, and her expression didn't alter, so I decided to throw caution to the wind. I stood and dusted myself down the best I could while thinking of the best way to respond.

She lived here alone, in this bleak forest. I guessed it could be beautiful here in the spring and summer, but now, in the thick of this sudden and monstrous winter, what sort of life could she be living? She appeared unhappy, her frown had etched itself deeply into her skin, and her eyes had sunk deeply into her face.

And if she was unhappy, and as Gwyn had suggested, responsible for this weather anomaly, how would she respond to kindness and warmth? Might that work?

I was at a loss. Nothing in my experience could prepare me for this, but I had to give it a go, so I took a deep breath.

"I wanted to come. I wanted to meet you."

Mara positively snarled at my words. "You were sent."

I shook my head. "No. It's not strictly true to say I was sent." I unzipped the top of my jacket and reached inside for the orb. I held it up so she could see it. For the first time, something in her eyes changed. Perhaps it was a trick of the light.

"This was given to me as a Christmas present by

my friend and mentor, Wizard Shadowmender. Do you know him?"

When Mara didn't reply, I continued, "But it was my great grandmother who thought I should pay a visit to you. If indeed you are who she thinks you are." The other witch leaned heavily on her stick and blinked once. I decided she would never admit to it but she wanted to know whom I was talking about.

"Her name is Alfhild Gwynfyre Daemonne, and she thinks you are called Mara and that she knew you when you were younger."

Silence stretched out between us. There was no sign of recognition on her part. No other movement from her. She remained cold and still and ultimately unreachable. I wondered desperately what else I could do. I took a step forward and that's when all hell broke loose.

Mara screamed at me again. "Stay back!" she shrieked and thumped her heavy stick against the ground.

The terrain beneath me wobbled and rolled and I lost my balance. When I tried to pick myself up, she hit the floor again. I couldn't right myself. Any movement from me and she cracked the stick. I hung on to the ground beneath me for dear life, riding a magic carpet of icy snow. The constant uneven jiggling made me nauseous until I could stand it no more.

"Please stop!" I called and heard her cackle with laughter. Mr Hoo glided towards her and she raised her stick to strike him.

"No," I screamed, and sent a beam of energy flying through the gulf between us, knocking the stick from her hand. It landed in the corner of her porch and she reached for it, easily calling it back. It flew through the air and she caught it smartly.

But then, abruptly, she stopped.

Panting with exertion, I squinted up at her, wondering what she was planning next. My stomach churned, and my head told me to get up and run hard in the opposite direction, but what I saw gave me pause.

She had cocked her head – listening. Fear—and something else I didn't comprehend at first—in her haunted eyes.

And then it clicked.

Desperation.

From the direction of the wooden cabin came a recognisable wail. A sound that called to every maternal instinct I possessed. A thin, weak cry. The mewling of a sick infant.

Without a second glance my way, Mara turned

on her heel and made a dash for the cabin, surprisingly light on her feet, given her advanced age. She pushed the door open and disappeared inside, leaving me alone to stare after her.

I could have upped and run. The ground had returned to its normal stable self, but the sky above darkened with every second, and the atmosphere filled with heavy foreboding. I recalled the look on Mara's face when she'd heard the cry from inside her home, and a sixth sense told me I couldn't leave yet.

So I picked myself up and I followed the elderly witch into the cabin.

CHAPTER SEVEN

I clambered up the slippery wooden steps to the porch that ran the length of the small cabin, trying to make as little noise as possible. Holding my breath, I pushed against the open door so that I could see what would await me if I walked inside.

The cabin was cold and shadowy. There appeared to be just the one room, with a large fireplace and range dominating the back wall. Normally it would provide heat and a place to cook, but today, a small fire burned without cheer, giving off a little light in the gloom but not much in the way of heat. Elsewhere I could make out a well-used kitchen table, and shelves galore, laden with coloured bottles and jars arranged neatly, each labelled in a spidery hand, while above my head, bunches of dried herbs and flowers jostled for space among hanging bags of ground spices and cured meats. On the far side of the room there was a large bench that doubled as seating and a bed, and arranged in front of the fire was a hand carved rocking chair, weathered with age.

The whole scene could have been cheerful, but dust and decay were evident everywhere. The cover on the bed was worn and filthy. The wood in need of a polish. The table had not been wiped down for a long time. The jars, cracked and crusted with filth were draped in old spider webs. It was a sad sight to behold.

But not as sad as the vision which drew my eye, centre stage.

Mara knelt at a raffia-woven bassinette, arranged in front of the fire. Her shaking hands reached for the squalling creature lying inside. With the utmost gentleness, she pulled a blanket slightly aside, and lovingly cupped the baby, lifting it clear of its swaddling and cradling it to her chest.

I halted where I was. Half in and half out of the cabin.

The baby was tiny. It couldn't have been more than a new-born, possibly even premature. I don't think I'd ever seen an infant as small, or even imagined one. If it weighed four or five pounds in weight, I'd have been surprised.

That the child was sickening seemed blindingly

obvious to me. There was no healthy rosy hue evident in this baby's cheeks. It was a grim shade of yellow, indicating jaundice or some other disease. It needed medical attention, and fast. I wanted to run over and grab the child from the witch, and then take to my heels across the snow, and race to the nearest human settlement to seek help.

But what stilled my hand was Mara, and the way she handled the baby with such consummate ease and experience. Every touch was loving and assured, her voice as she cooed to it, soothing and calm. The child's swaddling and blanket were clean and fresh, the bassinette old but pristine, the space they inhabited swept clean.

My gaze drifted across the scene, my brain struggling to understand what I was seeing, until aware that I was allowing the meagre warmth that existed in the cabin to seep out, I closed the door, drawing Mara's attention to me.

Her eyes were shining damply, tears flowing down her cheeks, pain etched into the deep crevices around her mouth.

"Whose baby is that?" I whispered. I could only assume she had stolen it. And very recently. A hideous crime.

Mara looked me directly in the eye and I read the heartbreak there. "It's my baby. It's mine."

I shook my head in disbelief. "It can't be, Mara. How is that possible?"

Her head dropped as she checked on the baby's wellbeing once more, then she carefully manoeuvred it so I could catch a clearer glimpse of it. I reached for the bundle, but Mara drew it back with a sharp shake of her head. When she held it out once more, I moved into the light so I could get a better look.

At first glimpse the baby appeared human, albeit underweight and poorly looking, but peering more closely at the sallow skin, so leathery beneath its blue Babygro, I could make out distinct features, slightly slanted eyes, ears with a point, a noble nose. This was no baby, but a faery.

I stared at the witch in confusion as she clasped the creature to her chest once more, clicking her tongue softly when it wailed, its cry unearthly and high-pitched.

I voiced my suspicions. "A changeling?" I asked and Mara nodded. "But how?"

Mara shrugged, and the creature let out another strangled cry.

"He doesn't have much time," she said softly.

"It's dying?"

"Yes." The sorrow carved into her features and the gravity and certainty of her tone broke my heart.

"Can I do anything?" I asked, panic bubbling just under the surface, feeling helpless.

She shook her head, and tears dripped down her nose and fell onto the baby's face. I welled up in sympathy, and dashed at my eyes with my gloved hand.

I couldn't give in to my feelings of empathy. I had to at least try and do something practical. I could start by warming the cabin up. I looked around for wood or coal but there was none by the hearth and the wood basket was empty. I exited the cabin. The wind was building up again, and the branches chimed above my head, clinking together, scattering tiny shards of icy glass around me. I looked up and shielded my eyes. I had never seen a daytime sky as darkly grey and foreboding as this one.

I located the wood pile to the right under a make shift shelter. Pulling my gloves off I checked for the driest wood, dragging an armful back to the fire. Mara and the bassinette were in the way, so I steered the former to the rocking chair, wrapped her up in the old bedcover from the bed, and moved the bassinette to her feet. She offered no resistance.

I built the fire up until it roared with life. The

cabin instantly warmed up and became cheerier. There was no food around, but I remembered my rucksack, and went off to locate it. My coming and going through the brambles and twisted undergrowth was much easier now that I had forged a path.

Back inside with Mara, I offered her soup from my thermos. At first she turned it down, but I kept on at her until she took some, and after that she seemed a little happier to accept some tea from me too. I set her kettle on the fire to heat up so that we had hot water.

The baby fretted and fussed and we looked down at him, her with love, me with wonder.

"Is there nothing we can do?"

"No," Mara replied, her voice so quiet I had to strain to hear. "It is Orin's time to depart this life. I will not see him again till we meet in the Summer Lands."

"How long does he – Orin – have?"

"I know not. But hours at the most."

I nodded my understanding. "Let me look after you both then." I put my hand out and smoothed the side of her face, wiping her tears away, and her mouth twitched, half-smile, half-helpless grimace.

For the next few hours, I cleaned the cabin

around her, while she sang ancient songs and rhymes to the baby in a strangely lyrical voice; pretty and lilting. Many of the songs were in a tongue I'd never heard before. I listened closely, while I washed shelves, wiped down bottles, dusted and swept. I kept the fire going, found candles and lit them, made endless cups of tea, joined in with a few nursery rhymes I knew, and all the while, a snow storm raged outside, buffeting the side of the cabin, icing over the windows, the wind whistling through the cracks in the door, and down the chimney.

Eventually there was no escaping the inevitable.

Orin's breathing had altered, become slow and erratic. We were out of time.

I drew up a stool and sat next to Mara, my hand placed gently on her thigh, so thin and bony beneath her robes. She sniffed noisily and hugged the tiny creature to her breast, drowning him in her tears.

"How come you came to have Orin?" I asked, curiosity getting the better of me. "Aren't changelings usually swapped for another baby?"

Mara glanced up at me, and nodded, her eyes ringed with red. She looked exhausted. "It was a mystery to me at the time. I had no baby. I've never had a child of my own. Rarely even an animal, apart from the odd raven." She blinked at Mr Hoo, whom I had allowed into the cabin when I was sure everything would be alright, and Mara wouldn't hurt him. He perched on the edge of the table, watching us warily, but no doubt glad to be inside on such an horrendous afternoon. "You're lucky," she continued. "You have a familiar. I've had nothing and no-one virtually my entire life. Do you have other family? Friends?"

I thought of my parents, both deceased, and then of the ghosts that kept me company at Whittle Inn. What were they if they weren't friends? And Charity of course. And then there was Wizard Shadowmender and all my friends and neighbours in the village. "I've lost some and I've gained some. I think I'm probably very lucky." I patted her knee. "But I've been lonely. Even very recently. I understand how you must feel."

"The loneliness ate me up for many years," Mara said. "I know I was tough to handle when I was younger. People found it difficult to co-exist with me or work with me. It's why I eventually found my way out here. By myself. It's easier to suffer loneliness when you're completely alone. Far harder to be the only lonely person among a room full of other people."

That made a certain amount of sense to me.

"But even here, the loneliness was hard to bear. Until one day I found the bassinette on the doorstep out there. I didn't know what to make of it at first. I knew it was a changeling. I figured it couldn't be for me. I would need to hand it back. And I wanted to. What did I need with an ugly old faery in my life?"

"So could you have given it back?"

"No. Well, I tried. I know where the Fae folk live here in this forest. Not too far away from here. There's one access point, at the centre of the forest, but I believe they have a vast underground cave network. They're mischief makers. They make the lives of the farmers nearby, hell. But then again, they don't bother me so I don't bother them. I took the baby and the bassinette back to them, but I couldn't get in to see them. Never made it further than the front gates."

"You went to the faery kingdom?" I asked.

Mara snorted. "The Fae folk here don't live in a kingdom. More like an underground fortress. Or an outpost, perhaps. Nonetheless, they wouldn't grant me access. I spoke to one of them. Urged him to appeal to the right person, but it got me precisely nowhere, so I came home with Orin and I've looked after him ever since."

"How long's that?"

"Getting on for a dozen years or so. Most changelings are elderly faeries the Fae are trying to rehome. Old soldiers and the like. They're swapped with human babies so they can live out the rest of their lives in peace and comfort, knowing only love. They maybe live a few weeks or months. Orin has kept me company for twelve wonderful years. I wouldn't have been without him. But now I'll have to be."

Now I understood the depth of Mara's grief. She had fallen in love with her faery child, and he, an ailing and aging soldier, had been her companion, a sorely needed friend for many years. Becoming a surrogate mother for a Fae child, had fulfilled a great need in Mara, and now she faced the rest of her life living alone, friendless and miserable.

No wonder her emotions were raging.

"One of their bigwigs visited me, about six months after Orin arrived here. Commander Warren I believe his name was. I worried they wanted Orin back, that they had realised their mistake. But he checked on Orin and left us to it."

She sighed and rocked Orin gently in her arms. "Everything was fine, until two days ago. He started failing." Fresh tears fell, "Oh Orin," she whispered to the little fellow. "I'll miss you for the rest of my life."

From outside I thought I heard a clap of thunder. Thunder in a snow storm? Could this get any worse. How on earth was I going to broach the subject of the weather and the problems it was causing in the outside world, when the poor woman in front of me was clearly broken hearted. Now was hardly the time to ask her to control her emotions.

I glanced nervously at Mara. Mara the Storm-bringer. She was well named.

Orin passed peacefully away thirty minutes later.

His breathing eased, and colour came back to his cheeks, but we recognised it as the final struggle for life, and Mara crooned to him as he breathed his last.

I helped her swaddle him from head to toe. She kissed his face, then covered him over and wrapped him all snuggly in his bassinette.

Then I held her while she howled for his loss, rocking in my embrace, while outside the bitterest winds in living memory whipped across the land-scape, locking down the countryside with iron-handed intensity.

CHAPTER EIGHT

The Fae folk arrived at midnight to collect their old soldier.

I had persuaded Mara to lie down on her bed, where she had cried herself to sleep, exhausted by the past few days of worrying and pre-grieving. I let her rest, stroking her back, feeling bone weary myself after a very long day.

When I had broached the subject of burying Orin, Mara had told me that he would be collected by his own kind. I somehow doubted they would venture out in this weather, but time quickly proved me wrong.

Having never seen a faery funeral before, this was quite a spectacle for me. They arrived in their dozens. I could hear them above the sound of the storm as they approached the cabin. They sang solemn songs in their own tongue, voices harmonising beautifully, and although I couldn't understand much of what they were saying, I guessed the content to be something along the lines of carrying their brother home.

I shook Mara awake, and she sat up groggily. Looking across at the bassinette, and hearing the ruckus outside, she instantly understood the situation. I helped her stand, handed her the tall stick she favoured, and we went to the front door to let the Fae folk in.

As Mara answered the imperious knock, I noted how the storm eased. Mara had control of herself, had contained her emotions for the time being, and therefore the adverse weather conditions were improving. She flung the door wide, and as if by magick – well indeed it was magick, Mara's magick – the skies cleared and stars blinked down from the heavens.

"Good Witch Mara?" A handsome faery, blonde hair cropped close to his head, standing just over a foot tall and wearing a ceremonial military uniform of red and blue, with shining blue buttons and a pill box hat set at a jaunty angle, stared up at her inquiringly.

"Yes," she answered. "Commander Warren?"

"The same. You remember," the faery sounded pleased.

"I do."

Commander Warren looked me up and down and decided I'd pass muster. He nodded my way, then dismissed me, turning his attention back to Mara.

Unfolding a roll of parchment, he cleared his throat and read, "Good Witch Mara. As you must appreciate, we are here to carry our comrade home. You, and I, indeed all of us, understood the day for this final journey would arrive. Orin had an illustrious career, and his retirement—with you—was equally glorious. And unexpectedly long. Now your work is complete, and we must gravely bear our responsibility to carry him out of the world we brought him into. However, I am bid by their magnificent and benevolent majesties, by the King and Queen of our beloved kingdom to convey their thanks to you, and to commend you for the care you so willingly and selflessly bestowed upon our beloved brother, Orin. It will never be forgotten. You are a true friend of the Fae folk."

Mara dabbed at her eyes, and I glanced out of the window to watch as snow began to fall from the sky once more.

"With that, we will bid you farewell, Good Witch Mara," Commander Warren finished, less officiously.

Mara nodded and stepped back, and several faeries entered the cabin and lifted Orin from the bassinette. They carried him carefully out of the door and transferred him to a litter. I followed Commander Warren and Mara out onto the porch behind the litter bearers, the biting night air pinching my cheeks. The faeries arranged themselves for a great procession. Some carried torches of fire, other sparkling lights of red and blue and green. When the litter was raised into the air, the assembled faeries— and there were dozens of them—let out a terrifying shriek that turned my insides to jelly. They set to with a great lament, a shrill warble, a vocal salute that acknowledged the passing of Orin from this world.

I swiped at my eyes, sniffling with empathy, absorbed in the grief so palpably displayed all around me.

As the Fae folk bore Orin away, I felt Mara shudder beside me, and then her pent-up grief erupted and she was howling again. The wind rushed at us, and a blizzard eclipsed the departing faery procession. I ushered her back into the cabin, and closed the door on the storm, pondering how I was going to ease Mara's grief.

In the early hours of Christmas day, I stared bleakly at the dying fire. Utterly exhausted, I'd been awake for nearly twenty-four hours. I opened my rucksack and ate the last of my squashed sandwiches. Behind me, Mara was curled on her side on her bed. I'd covered her in her blankets, and tried to soothe her, but the storm continued to rage outside and I knew I was having little effect.

It was blatantly obvious to me that I needed some sort of higher intervention.

As I sat and stared at the flames in the fire, I played through the events of the day. I considered Warren's words. What had he said to Mara? *He had been urged by the King and Queen of his beloved kingdom to convey their thanks to her, to commend her for her care.* But most importantly he had said, *it would never be forgotten.* "You are a true friend of the Fae folk."

If Warren had been sincere, surely they would help her?

But how would I find them? The storm outside

would have already obliterated any tracks they had left.

On a whim I picked up the orb, and held it in front of the fire to catch the light. The blizzard blew from left to right and right to left, and swirled around, before clearing. I could plainly see the long procession of Fae folk as they carried Orin home.

I swivelled in my seat, pointing the orb in the direction the faeries had taken.

And yes. There it was. Another star to follow.

CHAPTER NINE

The thought of making my way out into the biting wind and treacherous conditions didn't fill me with joy, but what else could I do? If I couldn't find a way to help Mara, who knew what kind of long-lasting damage her winter storm would wreak.

I thought of the community at Whittlecombe. With no power and just enough fuel to last for a few days, and only Rhona's little shop from which to replenish supplies, I genuinely feared for the well-being of the elderly and vulnerable. And what of the animals in the forest, in their burrows and nests, or out in the countryside in fields and barns? The farmers would be struggling in this weather. I couldn't have that on my conscience and not do anything.

And so regretfully, I tugged on my ripped down

jacket, my scarf, hat and gloves. I knotted the strap of my rucksack so that I could carry it again, and then looked thoughtfully at Mr Hoo.

"You know...it's hideous out there," I said to him. "You don't have to come. Perhaps you should stay here and wait for me to return."

Mr Hoo, perched on the back of the rocking chair near the fire, regarded me solemnly with his huge wise eyes, and didn't respond. I took that to mean he was happy to remain. A wise little fellow.

I glanced over at Mara and called to her, but she didn't respond. I knew she was awake. The wind howling around the sides of the cabin was testament to that. Throwing one last log on the fire, and nodding at Mr Hoo, I stepped out into the gale.

"Wish me luck," I said, but the words were whipped away by the ferocious wind no sooner than they were out of my mouth. I carefully closed the door and headed into the white-out.

The orb was a blessing. No two ways about it. I had no idea where I was in any case, but given that I could neither see nor hear anything, the going was treacherous. I held the orb at eye level and trusted the light inside to lead me where I needed to go. It was a little like water divining, some of which I had learned at school many years before, but with a pinprick of light rather than a pair of sticks. If I meandered off the path I needed, the light began to fail. If I remained vaguely on the right track, the light appeared small and yellow, but when I was heading in exactly the right direction, the light shone brilliant and white, and illuminated the blizzard of snow that leapt at me from every direction.

Nonetheless, even with a guiding light, the going was tough. The snow drifted into small mounds and larger hills. If I chose where to step poorly, I found myself flailing in piles of soft snow. I learned quickly to take everything slow and steady, and keep an eye on the light in the orb. For the most part it sent me along paths between rows of trees, where the snow wasn't as deep.

From time to time I thought I spied coloured lights ahead, evidence of the faery funeral procession, but whenever I blinked the snow out of my eyes, the lights would have disappeared again and I found myself completely alone once more.

The fourth time I face-planted in a mound of soft snow, I pushed myself to my knees, sore and stiff, coughing and sputtering like an old car, practically weeping with exhaustion. Time had been dragging, and I had no idea how long I'd been walking. It felt like an age. I considered turning about and retreating to the cabin, but my exhaustion disoriented me, and when I turned about, the orb only shone a light in one direction.

"Take me home," I told it, but nothing altered. I knew I could only travel forward to complete my mission.

There would be no going back.

I consoled myself with thoughts of the conversation Mara and I had shared. Hadn't she told me that the Fae folk had one access point in the centre of the forest? Shouldn't that mean that I couldn't be far from it? Unless the orb was sending me in the wrong direction.

Girded by this thought, I forced myself up and began walking again with purpose, and this time, when the brightly coloured lights glinted at me in the distance, I was sure I'd found the right path. My heart beat a little faster with an odd combination of joy and excitement, and I spurred my legs on with renewed energy. Surely this was journey's end?

Then the light in the orb disappeared and I was plunged into darkness.

I stopped in my tracks, rigid with shock. How could

the light in the orb have completely disappeared, unless I found myself in entirely the wrong place? This couldn't be happening.

"Oh no, oh no, oh no," I sang to myself. "What have I done? What have I done?" I shook the orb. "*Ostende mihi.*" My voice sounded querulous and weak in the darkness. *Intent*, I told myself. *Everything with intent.*

"*Ostende mihi,*" I commanded more fiercely, but still the orb remained lifeless in my hand.

I peered around, squinting into the darkness, but all that could be seen was the white of the snow in my immediate vicinity, whirling in front of my face, with total blackness beyond.

I stood still for some time, breathing raggedly, trying to quell the rising panic that churned in the pit of my stomach, but eventually I had to move. I couldn't remain in one place forever. I would freeze. I took a step forward, and collided with something spiky.

Screeching in fear, I dropped the orb. It landed in the soft snow at my feet, fortunately unbroken. Struggling to breathe, I held my hands out in front of me and tremulously reached out for the spiky things. They remained inert, although they weren't rock hard by any means. I twisted them and one or two snapped in my gloved hands. Holding them close to my face I could see they were tree roots.

I sighed with relief, my breath escaping jaggedly into the freezing air, huffs of white steam in front of my face. Surely there's nothing scary about a fallen tree?

Grabbing the orb in one hand, I felt my way along the side of the tree with the other. This was an enormous specimen. It had to have once been a mighty oak or a giant horse chestnut, because even lying on its side it stood taller than I. I walked gingerly, trailing my gloved hand along the trunk, until I came to the beginning of the massive crown. Although now stripped of leaves, the tree took up a wide expanse of ground.

I halted, wondering what to do next, and that's when the orb exploded into life once more, lighting up the surrounding areas by throwing a massive kaleidoscope of moving colour all around. This time, when I held my breath, it was to bask in the glory of a sensational rainbow prism, a silent firework display, and a meteor shower all rolled into one breath-taking extravaganza.

Even better, and much to my relief, I could clearly make out a path through the branches that led me to an opening in the ground. I had located the Faery fortress.

I found my way down a flight of worn stairs into a dimly lit cave. Several torches hung on the walls, but they burned low. The shadows were long, keeping secrets from strangers no doubt. Huge ornately carved wooden gates barricaded my way forwards.

It was a relief to be out of the howling wind and snow. My senses had taken a battering. My ears rang in the sudden silence, my eyes ached from straining to see, and I worried that my face—so numb with the cold—would ever feel sensation again.

With no other option open to me, I had to bang on the wooden gates. Almost immediately, a tiny peep hole opened, at about hip-height, to the side of me. A pair of bright eyes regarded me with sharp scrutiny.

"Who goes there?" A low voice.

I opened my mouth to speak, but my throat must have been frozen too, because for a moment no sound would escape. I cleared my throat and tried again. "My name is Alfhild Daemonne," I said huskily, trying to recapture some vocal strength. "I have followed Commander Warren and the funeral cortege from the Good Witch Mara's cabin in the woods, yonder."

The eyes continued to stare at me without blinking, but their owner remained mute.

I swallowed. "I would really like to talk to Commander Warren."

Still no response.

"Please."

There was a pause and then the flap slammed shut. The noise reverberated around the empty chamber. I waited for the gates to be opened, or for someone to shout to me, but nothing happened.

I waited and waited for what seemed an eternity, but no-one came, and there was no further response to my knocks on the wooden gate.

Shivering I retreated to the wall, out of the draught blowing down the stairs. I slunk to the floor, gripping my rucksack, the orb on the soft earth beside me.

Entirely alone, and my insides hollow, I found tears pricking at my eyes. I put my chin to my chest and tried to calm the dismal feelings of disappointment and failure, coursing through my insides.

I must have dozed because the next time I lifted my head, a small male faery, younger than the others I'd met previously, was regarding me with open disdain. Behind him, one of the gates stood open. He held a clipboard and a pen, and pointed the pen at the gate. "Shall we?" he asked. With some difficulty, I hoisted my stiff body from the floor, collected up my rucksack and the orb, and limped, stiff and tender, into an ante-chamber.

This had the same rough-hewn walls and earth floor, but here there were more torches and the flames burned brighter. A few plain wooden benches ran the length of two walls, and at the far end were another pair of wooden gates, heavily varnished and dark with age. On a slightly raised dais, off to the side, stood a plain oak table and heavy chair.

The faery indicated a bench and I sat.

"Alfhild Daemonne?" he asked, raising his eyebrows but staring at his clipboard.

"Yes."

He ticked a box. "And you're requesting an audience with Commander Warren?"

"Yes." Another tick.

"May I ask what your business is?" His pen poised in the air. My response would require more than a tick this time, I assumed.

"Well. Hmm. It's complicated," I said, wondering where to start.

"Commander Warren is an extremely busy man, Ms Daemonne. I'm sure you understand that. You will not be able to see him tonight, or indeed over the next few days. Far better that you leave now, and we will contact you when he has an opening."

A thought occurred to me. "Is he the head of the garrison here?"

"Certainly not," the faery chuckled, but more in scorn at my ignorance than amusement.

"Is he...very high up in the ranks?"

This time the faery looked at me, with an element of suspicion. He frowned, and didn't answer immediately.

Deciding to cut to the chase, I rushed on, "Only, I'm on a very important errand, and it is vital that I speak to someone who can help me. If it isn't Commander Warren, then I need to know who that person might be."

The faery sniffed and lay down his pen. I held his stare, watching him think. Eventually he tsk'd at me, and shook his head.

"It's impossible. Commander Warren will not see you."

But I could see I had gotten to him by

demanding he go higher up the echelons of power. Perhaps the situation had escalated beyond his pay grade. If indeed faeries were paid.

"Please wait," he instructed, and I settled back on the bench as he disappeared through the wooden gate into the garrison beyond.

When he returned, he had Commander Warren and several other high-ranking faeries in tow. I made the assumption they were high-ranking based on the fact that they too were wearing red and blue uniforms with lashings of gold insignia, as Commander Warren was.

I stood to greet them, weary to my bones.

"We meet again, Ms Daemonne." Commander Warren regarded me with curiosity. "Subaltern Ghosh tells me you require a meeting. How on earth did you find us? You couldn't possibly have followed us in this weather?"

"I'm very pleased to see you again, Commander Warren," I replied, for indeed I was. "I had help from this orb." I lifted it up so he could clearly see it.

He and the other faeries drew around me, and looked up at the glass ball with interest.

"Is this some sort of fortune telling ball?" one of them asked.

"I can't tell fortunes," I replied. "I use it as a kind of...sat-nav." I'd never thought of that before. I giggled, then roared with laughter.

"Hysteria," Subaltern Ghosh said knowingly, and the other faeries nodded.

I stifled my laughter, coughed self-consciously, and glared at Ghosh. Turning my attention back to the other faeries I explained, "It helps me find the way. Like a map. It shows me where to go."

"I can't see anything," Ghosh said.

I glowered at him again and pulled myself to my full height, a good few feet taller than him. "That doesn't mean that I can't."

"You're a witch," one of the other officers said, "like Mara?"

"Yes, a witch." I watched the faeries exchange glances. Witches and faeries muddled on together but often there wasn't a lot of love lost between us all.

"What on earth is so important that you have dragged yourself out on a night like this?" asked Commander Warren.

"Mara," I replied. "And the changeling. You have to know how important Orin was to her."

"Oh that." Warren smiled. "We can't help you with that." Turning on his heel he headed back towards the wooden gates. "Good day to you, Ms Daemonne." I was dismissed.

My heart sank. I had come all this way, to fail now would be unthinkable. I had to get through to these wretched faeries, but I couldn't think how.

I felt a vibration in my hand. Looking down I could see the orb glowing. I lifted it up to peer inside and light burst forth once more, throwing out an elongated and glittering golden beam that slid along the floor and climbed up the walls, and then quickly retreated back towards me, slowly shrinking in size but gaining in physicality and height, until at last it took a form, and stood tall and proud alongside me.

"Wizard Shadowmender!" I gasped, as the faeries whirled around in surprise.

"Greetings, Alf," he smiled. "I thought you might need some virtual assistance."

CHAPTER TEN

W izard Shadowmender had been the leader of my mother's coven while she lived. He'd also been a friend and mentor to me intermittently over the years, but particularly in the seven or eight months since my mother's death. He'd proven particularly useful in the aftermath of my inheritance of Whittle Inn (and several properties in and around the village of Whittlecombe) especially in light of the discovery of the body at Whittle Inn on my first day there.

He was a powerful wizard, revered in magickal circles. It had been largely thanks to Shadowmender that I had found my way back into the craft in the first place, and come to understood that my calling lay in what I liked to refer to as 'spiritual hospitality'—or food and drink at an inn full of ghosts. I owed a great deal to the wizard, and I was profoundly relieved to find him with me now.

Even if I didn't actually understand how he had manifested himself in the faery fortress.

He winked at me as if to say all would become clear, and then turned his attention to the Fae folk gathered in front of us.

"Commander Warren," said Shadowmender, his voice rich and melodic. "Commander Krevitz. Captain Bougnyne. Subaltern Ghosh. I apologise for not being here in person, but unfortunately the adverse weather conditions have made it difficult for these old bones to travel very far. Thank you for granting Alfhild your time and attention. I will of course return the favour at the earliest opportunity, should circumstances warrant."

Commander Warren, recovering his composure, smiled coolly at the wizard.

"Well met, Wizard Shadowmender. You too intend to petition us in regards to Mara, do you?"

"Certainly not. I would never meddle in the affairs of the Fae folk, you know that. Your rules, rituals and traditions are for your people alone, just as ours only apply to ourselves, and we would never encroach upon you or force you to fit our ways."

Warren nodded, his eyes flitting between Shadowmender and I. "Then...?"

"I ask only that you hear young Alfhild out. She has journeyed far in these extreme conditions, and her heart is warm. What harm can it do for you to listen to what she has to say?"

Warren sucked his teeth while the other faeries watched Shadowmender, their faces rapt. At last the Commander nodded curtly my way. "As you wish," he said.

I cast a sideways glance at Shadowmender then took a deep breath. "Thank you for hearing me out, kind sirs," I began. "The facts of the matter remain as you know them. The faery folk left a changeling with Mara the Stormbringer, around a dozen years ago. It was stated at the time, by yourself I believe Commander Warren, that it was a mistake. Orin was not swapped for a human baby, or even an animal one, as is the faery custom, but simply abandoned with Mara by mistake."

Commander Warren nodded curtly.

I shook my head. "I don't believe this is the truth."

Warren's eyes narrowed, and he looked at Shadowmender for clarification. Krevitz's brow furrowed. I understood I had committed a diplomatic faux pas, but I didn't care. I had to be heard. Ghosh gaped at me in alarm, but I pushed on.

"I've been giving this some thought, and do you know what I think? I think the garrison had been watching Mara for a while. You're all skilled soldiers and trained observers. You would have certainly kept a close eye on this woman when she moved into your territory. You might have been suspicious, given that she was a witch. You would have wanted to know what she was up to and why she chose to live so deep in the forest and away from civilisation.

"Without a doubt you would have started to notice her behaviours, and how her emotions affected the local weather conditions. Maybe in the beginning you would have seen a sudden squally shower here, or a fast moving storm there.

"But over time you would have equated the distress that Mara was experiencing with the weather. I'm certain of it. I think someone—perhaps you, Commander Warren—recognised how lonely Mara was. And I think you comprehended that by easing her loneliness, the Fae garrison would all live a more comfortable existence."

Warren opened his mouth to protest but I continued. "Perhaps it was just an experiment to begin with. Your changelings tend not to live long, after all. But Orin lived to a grand old age, and no doubt you all enjoyed the benign and balmy weather we've had of late."

The faeries muttered among themselves. Warren made a slight shrugging motion, hardly discernible underneath his bulging epaulettes.

"All I'm asking is that you consider Mara when you're placing another of your changelings. You know she would love him the way a mother loves a child, just as she did Orin."

"Mara is an old woman," Krevitz interrupted me, but I held out my hand in a gesture of appeasement.

"I know. And that is a good rebuttal. But she could live for years yet, and let's face it. Your changelings may only survive weeks or months. Consider Mara a foster carer, someone who will cherish them and meet all their needs."

"It's a risk we cannot take," Bougnyne muttered, and Krevitz twisted his mouth in agreement.

"It is a risk, but I give you my word that I will personally keep an eye on Mara. And if the worst should happen and Mara should pass while having the care of one of your retired soldiers, then I will take the changeling home to Whittle Inn and care for them myself."

There, I thought. *They can't ask for more than that, surely?*

Krevitz muttered something that I couldn't quite make out, and Warren cut him off. Turning to Shadowmender and myself he drew his heels together smartly. "Would you give us a moment to confer?" he asked, and I nodded.

"By all means," Shadowmender said.

I thought the faeries would leave but they huddled together on the dais talking in subdued tones. Krevitz spoke quickly and earnestly, and Warren answered him in measured tones. Bougnyne said very little, but occasionally glanced my way.

Eventually, the group split up and moved back in front of us.

"We have discussed your odd request," Warren said, "and regretfully find that we cannot acquiesce. We deny the insinuation that any changeling was placed with the Good Witch Mara, for any reason other than by mistake. The changeling system of care is one that the Faery kingdom take extremely seriously. It is therefore out of the question."

"But—"

"That is all," Subaltern Ghosh gushed, and I noted the gleam in his eye, the little weasel.

"By your leave," Commander Warren said, and

without waiting for a response, turned about and swept through the wooden doors and into the garrison beyond, carrying Commander Krevitz and Captain Bougnyne in his wake.

"Wait!" I called, catching the briefest glimpse of a long well-lit tunnel, an arched ceiling, boarded from tip to floor in sanded and varnished wood, hung with silk tapestries, but then the doors were closed and the bolts sent home. The deed was done.

Shadowmender and I regarded each other quietly.

"That didn't go as planned," I said, my heart sinking at the thought of Mara's grief and loneliness. I had failed her.

"Never give up hope, Alfhild. Where there is hope there is life." With that, the image of the wizard collapsed in on itself, shrinking to the size of a salt cellar and then with a distinct pop, disappeared altogether. The glow in the orb disappeared too, the glass cooling rapidly in my hand.

Ghosh picked up his clipboard from the desk and made a ticking motion on the page. I badly wanted to snatch the clipboard from his hands and either bash him over the head with it or throw it against the wall, but I resisted the urge. He looked up and regarded me with suspicion. I speculated whether he could read my mind the way Grandmama seemed to be able to. Then he indicated the heavy gates behind me. "If you please," he said, and ushered me through.

Once on the other side I turned to offer a final plea to Ghosh, but he rapidly back-pedalled away from me, the gates swinging closed as he went. "Good day to you," he called, motioning to someone out of my sight line, disappearing from view as the gates fully locked into position once more.

I turned about. Alone once more.

Bleakly I climbed the steps, up into the white winter wonderland that awaited me. Dawn was breaking, and through the trees it was difficult to know where the white of the snow finished and the white of the sky began. The landscape was unrecognisable. Twisted skeletal trees pointed me in every direction, but there were no other landmarks to offer clues. I held the orb up and looked for a light, turning it around and about, and upside down.

"Show me the way to Mara," I instructed it, but it lay inert on my gloved hand, no blizzard and no stars. It had become nothing more than a large glass marble.

Which way should I go? Any footprints I had left here had long since been covered over. Turning my face into a fresh flurry, I shivered with cold. Any way at all was better than no way. I needed to keep moving.

At that moment the soft thrum of beating wings passed by my right ear. My teeth chattered as I looked up in hope, then smiling to see a familiar friend alight on a branch above my head.

"Hoo-ooo," he called. "Hoo-ooo."

"Show me the way," I said, mentally reaching out to lean on Mr Hoo.

All was not lost.

Just as Shadowmender had said. Where there is hope, there is life.

CHAPTER ELEVEN

Perhaps it was my imagination, but the storm appeared to be easing by the time we made it back to Mara's cabin. Or maybe the wind had merely worn itself out, and the clouds had given up as much snow as they could manage for the time being. I climbed tiredly up the steps and softly knocked on the door, before letting myself in.

The fire had burned down, and the candles had gone out, nonetheless the pale light outside showed me that Mara remained exactly where I had left her in the early hours of the morning, huddled on her bed with her back to the door.

I tip-toed across, fearful of waking her if she slept, but she lay with her eyes open, tears oozing from their corners.

I touched her shoulder gently. "It's me, Mara. I've come back. Let me make you some breakfast." I let her be, while I stripped off my outer layers, and then bustled around, building the fire up and boiling water, before setting tea to brew in a chipped old tea pot. There was nothing in the cabin I could utilise to make us breakfast. I would have to head back to the inn and then return with provisions.

The thought filled me with gloom.

I had to do right by her, but it would be easier if I could travel at least part of the way by road. I wondered how long it would be before Mara's grief would ease, and thereby allow the weather to improve, but I recognised there was no hurrying the way she felt. I could only hope she didn't get worse.

I helped her up, and sat her in the rocking chair next to the fire, wrapping her bedcover around her, while she nursed her black tea. At least the warm drink seemed to bring a little colour into her cheeks. I hated the loneliness I saw in her eyes, and recognised in her the fear that stemmed from being alone.

She glanced at the empty bassinette as ice spattered against the window. The storm appeared to be building again.

"Mara," I said, sitting next to her on the stool and patting her arm. "I'm going to have to return to the inn. But I'm worried about you. You have nothing here to eat. If I leave you alone how do I know you'll keep yourself warm?"

She stared at me, her eyes dark and lost.

"I want you to come with me. Will you do that?"

I thought she wouldn't answer, but she turned her head to stare at the window, and the way the ice glazed over the top, blurring the view of the trees outside. "We'd never make it, Alf my dear."

Her affectionate turn of phrase, coupled with her mournful tone, twisted a knife in my heart. She liked me. That was a good sign. I wouldn't leave her here by herself, come hell or high water.

"We will make it. We must. I won't leave you here alone, Mara. I'm your friend. You'll find new friends with me at Whittle Inn. You'll love it, I promise. It's a silly old wonky building, all bent out of shape with age. I can take care of you. You can help me with the garden."

She offered a kind-of half-smile. "It sounds lovely, Alf, but...I belong here. I can't get through the storm."

I shook my head, desperately. "You can get through the storm. You can stop the storm, Mara. You know that. It's all in your head. If you...I don't know...think positive...if you conjure up the sun or something, then we'll both make it through."

She shook her head obstinately and I slumped on the stool, wondering what I could do or say next to persuade her to come with me. I couldn't physically carry her all the way to Whittlecombe through both the forest and Speckled Wood.

The distant clamour of twinkling bells caught my attention. I listened closely, and the noise came again. Light and jolly. Seasonal. A sound you might associate with the reindeer on Santa's sleigh. Closer it travelled, at once fantastical, and yet at the same time, oddly familiar at this time of year. Certainly not even slightly out of place in the current wintery conditions.

I stood, trying to peer outside through the ice-mottled window, and as I did the world beyond exploded with light. A colourful and glittering display —in neon pink, the brightest of blues, the sunniest of yellows, the zingiest green and zestiest orange— zapped the cottage, melting the ice from the windows. At the same time, the rapid clump of feet on the porch outside reached the door and then, just as quickly, retreated. The bells tinkled once more, there came another blinding flash, and finally a whoosh.

I hurried to the door and flung it open, the sounds of the jingling bells still disappearing in the distance. I imagined I caught sight of the rear end of a small sleigh, but everything happened so quickly, I couldn't be sure.

I took a step forward, to get a closer look, and nearly trod on a bundle of rags that had blown on to the step.

It stirred, and a tiny cry escaped from somewhere within.

Aghast, and wondering whether an animal had somehow gotten trapped in waste, I knelt down to investigate. The bundle had been arranged on a mattress of straw, no more than a foot in length, and something seemed to be wriggling in the midst of the pile.

The cry came again. A mewling pitiful cry and now I knew for certain what I'd found.

I reached forward to free it, when Mara suddenly shot past me and knocked my hand away.

"Careful my girl! Easy now."

The old witch knelt beside me, and with the gentle ministering touch I had seen her use on Orin, she parted the cloth until a bright pink screwed-up face emerged. I sucked my breath in. A tiny baby, perfect in every way.

Except as Mara tenderly lifted the child clear of

its rags, I clearly saw the leathery worn face of an aging Fae soldier.

I shot a look in the direction I had imagined the sleigh had taken. No tracks. It had to be the faeries. Heading back towards the garrison, no doubt.

Beside me, Mara cooed, tears in her eyes. I blinked rapidly myself.

"Commander Warren, you old dog," I muttered, shaking my head in disbelief. "I take my hat off to you. You've made a pair of witches very happy."

Mara relaxed by the fire in her rocking chair, feeding the changeling the remains of her cup of tea from a teaspoon.

"I can't keep him," she was saying. "What were they thinking of?

I jabbed at the fire with the poker and rolled my tired eyes. We'd been having this conversation for the past thirty minutes. "You have to keep him, Mara. I'm fairly sure no-one is going to take him away from you. They're not going to send anyone to collect him either. You know what the Fae are like, they never own up to their mistakes."

"Well I'm surprised at them if I'm honest," Mara

lifted the faery to her shoulder and patted his back. He burped contentedly. It was disconcerting to hear a deep old man's belch from such a small baby-like figure. I pulled a disgusted face then had a quiet giggle to myself.

"It's unlike the fastidious faery folk to make the same mistake twice. They're sticklers for order and routine and following the rules," Mara explained, a slight frown on her otherwise shining face.

"They are, that," I agreed, keeping myself busy and trying not to look at her for fear of giving myself away.

"I'm not going to love this little fellow," she continued, tucking him carefully around her soft old bosom, wrapped in Orin's clean fleece blanket. He snuggled contentedly into her and she chucked him under the chin with a smile.

"No, okay, I can see that." I hid my smirk.

"He'll have to go back." She rocked him gently.

"Alright. I'll attend to it then." I had absolutely no intention of going back to the garrison ever again if I could help it.

A sudden rumble above my head caused me to look up in alarm, fearing a faery drone strike or attack by some other supernatural creature. It was followed almost immediately by a loud thud at the side of the cabin. Crying out, imagining Warren had changed his mind or the other faeries disagreed with his decision to bring the changeling to Mara, or something even worse, I dashed for the door and threw it open, ready to fight whatever demons were threatening our quiet idyll. What I saw there halted me instantly in my tracks.

The sound I'd heard was snow on the roof of the cabin sliding off and crashing to the ground alongside the porch. The winter world I had become so accustomed to over the past few days...was melting. The ice on the tree branches had liquefied and was dripping steadily into the snow below, causing exaggerated snow holes to appear beneath the trees. The drifts themselves had started to shrink. From close by came the musical tinkle of running water, the forest zipped and sang with the energy of small mammals as they ventured from their hiding places deep in the freezing earth. And then suddenly, because the forest had abruptly come alive again, the birds began calling to each other, and the joyful sound of blackbirds singing filled the air.

Finally Mara had calmed down enough to enable the English winter to continue at its usual tepid pace. She had re-found her sense of self, and grounded herself in reality. Her love for the new changeling, warmed even her frosty old heart.

Mr Hoo fluttered out of the cabin and settled on the corner of the railing at the top of the steps. I reached out to stroke his soft ears.

"Hoo-oo," he gave a sweet little owly head wobble and I laughed at his cuteness.

"Merry Christmas to you too, my darling little friend."

CHAPTER TWELVE

I couldn't persuade Mara to return to the inn with me, no matter how I tried, but I promised to send provisions. The rapid thaw would make it easier for me to walk back to the inn - swelling brooks, fords and rivers allowing - and then I could arrange transportation of whatever Mara needed and either send it out with Stan from the shop, or bring it myself by road.

"You should change your mind, Mara," I said. We stood at the door of the cabin and I hugged her as I bid her farewell. "Even if you only stay a day or two. I can feed you up and pamper you at the inn. Come with me. Both of you."

"No, my girl. You're kind to old Mara, but I have to make arrangements to send this changeling back to the faeries." She glanced over her shoulder fondly, checking on his well-being. He chortled in the bassinette by the fire, and I could tell Mara was itching to get back to him.

"Very well," I said, and squeezed her thin frame once more before waving goodbye.

Although squidgy underfoot, the return walk through the forest was much easier than the original journey had been, just over 24 hours before. I hadn't slept a wink, except for an unplanned doze at the faery garrison, and I was shattered. I turned my nose for home, and placed my back to the sun, heading south west. The orb, silent and still, remained stowed in my tatty rucksack.

As I marched home, I reflected on how things could have been if this particular adventure had ended differently. Would I have made it back to the inn in one piece without freezing to death? Would my body have ever been found? Would Yetis have taken residence in the East Devon countryside?

It didn't bear thinking about.

The one thing that pleased me however, was that the further my tired feet took me, the less snow there was on the ground, the bluer the sky, the fewer the clouds, and the warmer the sun on my back.

By the time Mr Hoo and I reached the outskirts of Speckled Wood, I had pulled off my jacket and tied the arms around my waist.

Phew. Mara had to be the happiest witch in the region, because this was going to be the warmest Christmas on record.

I stumbled through the back door of Whittle Inn just after midday. Florence, Monsieur Emietter, and several of the Wonky Inn Clean-up Crew were in residence, flying around the kitchen, busily chopping, stirring, agitating, spreading, creaming, smoothing, sponging, roasting and baking. The smell—you can imagine—could only be described as heavenly.

My stomach growled with hunger as I stood at the door basking in the sights and scents.

"Miss Alf," Florence said excitedly when she spotted me, "It's so good to have you back. We've all been worried about you, although your Grandmama said you would return, and she knows such things."

"Does she indeed?" I asked. Good to know that my great grandmother had every confidence in me.

Charity burst into the kitchen waving a sheet of paper. "Monsieur Emietter. I have a guest with coeliac disease," she began, but stopped when she saw me. "Alf," she screeched, so loudly that Monsieur Emietter covered his ears and tutted loudly.

"*Sacre bleue!*"

"For heaven's sake, Alf!" Charity blithely ignored the crotchety old chef. "Where have you been? The electricity is still out in the village and I have dozens of guests here for lunch. Apparently you invited everyone!"

"Did I?" I asked, trying to recall. "Oh I suppose I did." I looked around at all the busy hands. "We can cope, right? We have enough food?"

"Well, yes, with a little effort. I don't think we'll all be sitting down for lunch much before four though."

"That's fine." I smiled. "No-one will mind. Maybe sort out some games to keep people amused? Perhaps some non-alcoholic cocktails for the next few hours? We don't want people to peak too early."

A bell rang in the bar and Charity tutted. "That must be someone else arriving." She blew bright pink hair from her hot brow but then caught my eye and winked. She was having the time of her life. It was wonderful to have the inn full of guests at Christmas.

"Go," I said and shooed her away. "I need to nip upstairs and clean myself up. I'll be down in a bit."

"You look exhausted," Charity said, with genuine concern.

"Don't worry. I'll borrow some of Grandmama's magick make-up. I'll look like I've just returned from two weeks in the Caribbean very shortly. Mark my words."

The bell rang again and Charity emitted a little squeak before dashing away. I stood in the middle of the kitchen and snapped up a naked vanilla cupcake when a tray of them floated past me on the way to the decorating table. Monsieur Emietter scowled at me, never fond of having interlopers in his kitchen, and I smiled happily.

Oh, it was good to be home!

I'd like to say I made a grand entrance to my own Christmas party a little while later, but given my general exhaustion, it was no surprise when I tripped on the hem of my long black skirt on the stairs and fell down the last few steps. There were gasps and titters, and Grandmama rolled her eyes at my lack of grace.

George Gilchrist came to my rescue.

"Hey," I said, clasping the detective's hand and pulling myself up. "I wasn't expecting you here today." George and I were building a little personal history together, in a slow and civilised way. Memories of Jed, from my early days at the inn were still raw for me.

He pulled me into a close embrace, hugged me, and kissed my forehead. "I had a call from Charity yesterday morning. She was frantic when you disappeared. And let's face it, the weather was atrocious. She had every right to be worried. I borrowed the 4 x 4 from work—we have snow chains—and came directly over."

"And let me guess," I said stealing a glance at Gwyn, who appeared to be regaling some older members of the Whittlecombe community, with stories from her youth. Back in the dark ages. "Grandmama persuaded you everything would be fine."

"She did," George said. "But I still went out looking for you."

I met his eyes, and my heart tilted in shy happiness. George Gilchrist was a good man, a handsome man, and I was a lucky woman.

"I've left a gift for you next to the fire," George

said. "Make sure no-one else nabs it. Let me get you a drink. Champagne?"

"Thank you! Just a small one," I said and darted away to hunt excitedly for my present among the small pile collected at the foot of the hearth. I sifted through them and found a small one that could only have been jewellery of some kind, given the size and shape of the box. Smiling I turned the bauble-styled label over to read the message.

Alf, it read, *you're never far from my thoughts. Love always, Jed.*

My stomach dropped as though I was riding an express elevator.

Jed.

I flipped the label over. Purposefully chosen. A red bauble, with gold glitter stuck to it. The Mori. They were watching me still. Perhaps waiting for the time they could exact revenge.

Without thinking, I threw the gift into the fire. "*Perdere!*" I spat and the fire hissed back at me, the small parcel crumpling in on itself and disappearing with a pop. I watched it, calming my nerves, stilling my shaky breathing.

George Gilchrist's beautifully wrapped package lay at my feet, much larger, squidgy, and somehow less presumptive. I would open it later. The moment had been spoilt for me.

At that instant the front door bell clanged once more. I caught Charity's eye across the crowded room. She carried a tray of drinks and was busily weaving in and out among our guests and ghosts. I mouthed "I'll go," at her, and made my way to the front door of the inn.

Throwing it open, I beamed in delight. Standing there smiling right back at me, her hair freshly washed and pinned up in a neat bun, her face shining with happiness, was Mara. The changeling was nestled against her chest in a large shawl she'd folded into a sling, its eyes closed, snoring contentedly. She hadn't returned it to the faery fortress after all.

"Mara!" I cried and reached forward to usher her inside. "Welcome to my wonky inn! We are thrilled to have you here."

Mara hovered close to the door, looking around in wonder. Dozens of candles—lit to mask the absence of electricity—sparkled in the glass and mirrors around the bar. The room hummed with more people than Mara had seen in many years. She appeared slightly taken aback, and I sensed a little panic.

"It will be fine," I soothed her. "I'll introduce you to a few people, and you needn't feel overwhelmed. You can escape to one of the bedrooms if you need to, or if it gets too much for..." I indicated the changeling.

"Harys," she said, nodding gratefully.

I stood on tiptoes and waved at Gwyn.

At first my great grandmother tried to ignore me, but eventually, when I became more overt in my gesturing, so much so that others were noticing, she had to look my way. When she recognised Mara I saw her mouth drop open in surprise. She wafted over to us hurriedly, her long ball gown trailing across the floor, and greeted Mara like an old friend. Mara seemed happy to see someone she vaguely knew too, and the pair of them clucked over the changeling like competing grandparents.

Charity wandered over with her tray, and I asked her to show Mara to a bedroom, where she could hang-out alone if the need arose.

Gwyn stood next to me as we watched them disappear up the stairs.

"My goodness, Alfhild," Grandmama said, her voice full of rare approval. "That was a job well done. I can't believe you managed to rescue the witch who killed Christmas, and turn the situation right around. Impressive, darling."

I glanced about the bar. Mr Hoo perched on the mantle above the fire, plucking stray feathers from himself. Some of my best friends—Millicent, Rhona, Stan and Sally, not to mention George and the ghosts —were singing Greensleeves at Luppitt Smeatharpe's insistence, while he strummed his lute and conducted them all.

My wonky inn was warm and full of the scents of roasting meat, sweet cinnamon, honey and orange. At that moment I knew a happiness so deep and fulfilling I could have burst.

"But she didn't kill Christmas, did she?" I asked. "She didn't even come close."

The End

Jeannie Wycherley
East Devon
31st October 2018

NEED MORE WONKY?

The story begins...

The Wonkiest Witch: Wonky Inn Book 1

Alfhild Daemonne has inherited an inn.
And a dead body.

Estranged from her witch mother, and having committed to little in her thirty years, Alf surprises herself when she decides to start a new life.

She heads deep into the English countryside intent on making a success of the once popular inn. However, discovering the murder throws her a curve ball. Especially when she suspects dark magick.

Additionally, a less than warm welcome from several

locals, persuades her that a variety of folk – of both the mortal and magickal persuasions – have it in for her.

The dilapidated inn presents a huge challenge for Alf. Uncertain who to trust, she considers calling time on the venture.

Should she pack her bags and head back to London? Don't be daft.

Alf's magickal powers may be as wonky as the inn, but she's dead set on finding the murderer.

Once a witch always a witch, and this one is fighting back.

A clean and cozy witch mystery.

Take the opportunity to immerse yourself in this fantastic new witch mystery series, from the author of the award-winning novel, Crone.

Grab Book 1 of the Wonky Inn series, The Wonkiest Witch, right here

EVEN MORE WONKY?

The series continues in Wonky Inn Book 2 – The Ghosts of Wonky Inn

Alf has tried to banish her demons.

And her ghosts.

But memories of Jed linger and keep her awake. Every night it's the same. When she does eventually drift off, she's woken almost immediately by a sobbing spirit.

He's lost. And worse than that, someone is trying to kill him.

Who is this sad specimen of a spirit? And where does he belong?

And how do you kill someone ... who is already dead?

Find out what Alf gets up to next.

Pre-order The Ghosts of Wonky Inn here

WONKY INN BOOK 3

Fancy a Wonky Inn story with added bite?

Try Weird Wedding at Wonky Inn

Whittlecombe.

A charming and peaceful village in the south west of England. All thatched cottages and winding country lanes, triangle sandwiches and cream teas.

Picture postcard perfection in fact.

But people are dropping like flies.

Wonkiest witch, Alfhild Daemonne, is just about to host the vampire wedding of the century at Whittle Inn.

Coincidence?

Are Alf's fangtastic guests to blame? Or could bitter arch rivals 'The Mori' be making a move on Alf and her wonky inn once more?

Read the latest of Alf's adventures, Weird Wedding at Wonky Inn, right here!

Please consider leaving a review?

If you have enjoyed reading The Witch Who Killed Christmas, please consider leaving me a review.

Reviews help to spread the word about my writing, which takes me a step closer to my dream of writing full time.

If you are kind enough to leave a review, please also consider joining my Author Street Team on Facebook – Jeannie Wycherley's Fiendish Street Team. Do let me know you left a review when you apply because it's a closed group. You can find my fiendish team at https://www.facebook.com/groups/JeannieWycherleysFiends/

You'll have the chance to Beta read and get your hands on advanced review eBook copies from time to time. I also appreciate your input when I need some help with covers, blurbs etc.

Or sign up for my newsletter http://eepurl.com/cN3Q6L to keep up to date with what I'm doing next!

ACKNOWLEDGEMENTS

This little story was so much fun to write, and I am really enjoying continuing my love affair with Alf and her friends.

Huge thanks as always to my growing street team: Jeannie Wycherley's Fiendish Author Street Team, for their engagement and support. Shout outs to Debbie Alvarado and the ladies in her book club all the way over the pond in Texas, Rosemary Kenney, Heaven Riendeau, Bax Al, Morag Fowler, Rachel Barton, Nina Hesslewood, Roxanne Glawson, Rob Parker, Irene O'Brien, Sandra Tickner-Hobson, among others.

Special thanks to JC Clarke of The Graphics Shed for her phenomenal covers, and to Anna Bloom, for her passion and her belief.

Finally, most importantly, thanks to you, the reader. I love bringing you my stories, reading your reviews, and receiving your feedback. You complete my circle.

Much love ♥

Jeannie Wycherley
Devon, UK
31st October 2018

THE WONKY INN SERIES

The Wonky Inn Series
The Wonkiest Witch: Wonky Inn Book 1
The Ghosts of Wonky Inn: Wonky Inn Book 2
Weird Wedding: Wonky Inn Book 3
Fearful Fortunes and Terrible Tarot: Wonky Inn Book 4 Due for release 31st January 2019
The Mystery of the Marsh Malaise: Wonky Inn Book 5 Due for release 28th February 2019
The Witch Who Killed Christmas: Wonky Inn Christmas Special

ALSO BY

Beyond the Veil (2018)

Crone (2017)

A Concerto for the Dead and Dying (short story, 2018)

Deadly Encounters: A collection of short stories (2017)

Keepers of the Flame: A love story (Novella, 2018)

Non Fiction

Losing my best Friend Thoughtful support for those affected by dog bereavement or pet loss (2017)

Follow Jeannie Wycherley

Find out more at on the website
www.jeanniewycherley.co.uk

You can tweet Jeannie twitter.com/Thecushionlady

Or visit her on Facebook for her fiction
www.facebook.com/jeanniewycherley

Sign up for Jeannie's newsletter
http://eepurl.com/cN3Q6L

COMING SPRING 2019

The Municipality of Lost Souls by Jeannie Wycherley

Described as a cross between Daphne Du Maurier's *Jamaica Inn*, and TV's *The Walking Dead*, but with ghosts instead of zombies, *The Municipality of Lost Souls* tells the story of Amelia Fliss and her cousin Agatha Wick.

In the otherwise quiet municipality of Durscombe, the inhabitants of the small seaside town harbour a deadly secret.

Amelia Fliss, wife of a wealthy merchant, is the lone voice who speaks out against the deadly practice of the wrecking and plundering of ships on the rocks in Lyme bay, but no-one appears to be listening to her.

As evil and malcontent spread like cholera throughout the community, and the locals point fingers and vow to take vengeance against outsiders, the dead take it upon themselves to end a barbaric tradition the living seem to lack the will to stop.

Set in Devon in the UK during the 1860s, *The Municipality of Lost Souls* is a Victorian Gothic ghost story, with characters who will leave their mark on you forever.

If you enjoyed *Beyond the Veil*, you really don't want to miss this novel.

Sign up for my newsletter or join my Facebook group today.

Printed in Poland
by Amazon Fulfillment
Poland Sp. z o.o., Wrocław

77317305R00087